"Move in with me, Sara."

Her mouth fell open. Those were the last words she'd have expected to come from Nat's mouth. "I can't stay with you."

"People move in with people they don't know all the time," he said.

He was right, of course. But she couldn't do it. Not with Nat. It would be awkward...and the strange awareness between them might intensify.

She had to be nuts for even thinking about taking him up on his offer.

"People will talk."

"Probably."

Not that he cared what people thought of him. And it would only be for the summer. "Are you sure you want us, Nat?"

"I'll keep the both of you safe."

Dear Harlequin Intrigue Reader,

We have another month of spine-tingling romantic thrillers lined up for you—starting with the much anticipated second book in Joanna Wayne's tantalizing miniseries duo, HIDDEN PASSIONS: FULL MOON MADNESS. In *Just Before Dawn,* a reclusive mountain man vows to get to the bottom of a single mother's terrifying nightmares before darkness closes in.

Award-winning author Leigh Riker makes an exciting debut in the Harlequin Intrigue line this May with *Double Take.* Next, pulses race out of control in *Mask of a Hunter* by Sylvie Kurtz—the second installment in THE SEEKERS—when a tough operative's cover story as doting lover to a pretty librarian threatens to blow up.

Be there from the beginning of our brand-new in-line continuity, SHOTGUN SALLYS! In this exciting trilogy, three young women friends uncover a scandal in the town of Mustang Valley, Texas, that puts their lives—and the lives of the men they love—on the line. Don't miss *Out for Justice* by Susan Kearney.

To wrap up a month of can't-miss romantic suspense, Doreen Roberts debuts in the Harlequin Intrigue line with *Official Duty,* the next title in our COWBOY COPS thematic promotion. It's a double-murder investigation that forces a woman out of hiding to face her perilous past…and her pent-up feelings for the sexy sheriff who still has her heart in custody. Last but certainly not least, *Emergency Contact* by Susan Peterson—part of our DEAD BOLT promotion—is an edgy psychological thriller about a traumatized amnesiac who may have been brainwashed to do the unthinkable….

Enjoy all our selections this month!

Sincerely,

Denise O'Sullivan
Senior Editor,
Harlequin Intrigue

JUST BEFORE DAWN

JOANNA WAYNE

HARLEQUIN®

TORONTO • NEW YORK • LONDON
AMSTERDAM • PARIS • SYDNEY • HAMBURG
STOCKHOLM • ATHENS • TOKYO • MILAN • MADRID
PRAGUE • WARSAW • BUDAPEST • AUCKLAND

ISBN 0-373-22771-X

JUST BEFORE DAWN

ABOUT THE AUTHOR

Joanna Wayne lives with her husband just a few miles from steamy, exciting New Orleans, but her home is the perfect writer's hideaway. A lazy bayou, complete with graceful herons, colorful wood ducks and an occasional alligator, winds just below her back garden. When not creating tales of spine-tingling suspense and heartwarming romance, she enjoys reading, traveling, playing golf and spending time with family and friends.

Joanna believes that one of the special joys of writing is knowing that her stories have brought enjoyment to or somehow touched the lives of her readers. You can write Joanna at P.O. Box 2851, Harvey, LA 70059-2851.

Books by Joanna Wayne

*Randolph Family Ties
†Hidden Passions
**Hidden Passions: Full Moon Madness

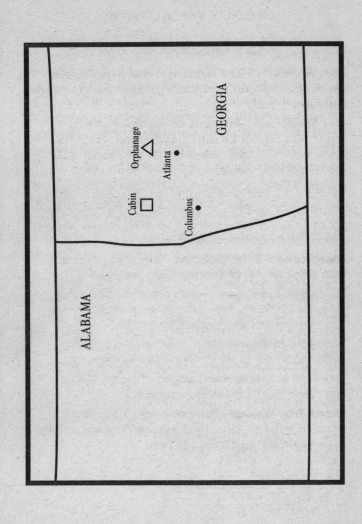

CAST OF CHARACTERS

Sara Murdoch—The nightmares that have plagued her since childhood have suddenly taken a frighteningly real turn.

Nat Sanderson—He came to the mountains to forget his past, but he can't stand by and watch his lovely neighbor suffer when he has the special skills she desperately needs.

Kendra Murdoch—Sara's precocious four-year-old has an alarming habit of making friends with strangers.

Judge Cary Arnold—Has the prominent judge enjoyed success over someone's dead body?

Mattie and Henry Callahan—The loving couple have a helpful way of minding everyone's business.

Dr. Abigail Harrington—Sara remembers her as a kind and helpful therapist. But is her purpose to help Sara remember, or to ensure she forgets?

Raye Ann Jackson—Sara's dear friend would do anything to help Sara—if she could only wake up.

Jack Trotter and Bruce Dagger—The FBI agents don't appear on any Bureau payroll list.

Sheriff Troy Wesley—For a man who supposedly wants to solve his case, the local sheriff seems awfully determined not to accept any help.

To Randy, Gail, Chase and Jameson, who always make our visits to Georgia such a delightful experience. And a special nod of appreciation to the hospitable folks of north Georgia for making the research so much fun. And hugs to my hubby for hiking mountain trails with me when he'd much rather have been golfing.

Prologue

Craig Moffitt mopped a salty stream of sweat from his brow with a bleached white handkerchief, then stuffed the soaking square of threadbare cotton into his back pocket. Demolition was hell on the system anytime of the year, but it was downright criminal in the heat of a Georgia summer. 'Course, late May was officially spring but you wouldn't know it by the temperature. High eighties already and it wasn't even noon yet. And they were in the mountains, almost to Tennessee. He hated to think how hot it was down in Atlanta.

"'Bout all I can do with the bulldozer," Gus called. "Reckon we'll have to take the rest of her out with picks and shovels."

"Can't see why we have to bother. Place is already leveled. Nothing left but the basement. The guy can just fill her up with dirt and let her go. What's a few bricks left under the ground?"

"Boss said the new owner don't want no sign the building ever stood on his property. Says it's an abomination."

"Building was a church for Pete's sake. An orphanage after that. Don't see how a man with half a heart can call either of those an abomination.''

"He's paying. He can do the calling, lessen you want to hang around and tell him different.''

"It's just a job to me. If I'm not sweating and straining here, I'll be doing it somewheres else.'' Craig turned to the rest of the crew, such as it was. A couple of college guys working to earn spending money and Jimmy, a new guy with way more brawn than brains.

"You guys grab some picks out of the back of the truck. Jimmy, you get the jackhammer and 'tach it to the gas engine. Let's take out that basement wall.''

The college boys shrugged their shoulders and took their own sweet time about it. Jimmy smiled as he headed toward the jackhammer.

Craig walked over to the truck, pulled a soda out of the cooler, screwed off the top and gulped it down. He was almost back to the basement site when he heard Jimmy let out a string of curse words.

"You got a problem?'' Craig asked, peering into the dank hole of crumbling brick and mildewed earth.

"I got more than that. I got a skull.''

He held it up for the rest of them to see.

"Looks mighty small,'' Gus said, jumping into the hole. "Had to be a baby.''

Jimmy reached into the hole the skull had tumbled from. This time he pulled out a bone that looked to be part of a tiny spine.

One of the college boys tugged on a loose brick and a whole slew of bricks started falling. Craig jumped out of the way just as a second skull rolled across the broken cement and wedged between his boot and the wall.

"I'm not digging in no graveyard," Jimmy said, backing away. "It's unholy."

"Weren't no grave site here," Gus said. "Just a church and an orphanage. Not supposed to be any dead babies here for sure. Reckon I better call the sheriff."

Craig backed away from the skull. He felt weird inside, like his insides were all gritty and dirty, the same as his trousers were. He was a little scared, too, and he didn't get scared often.

"You guys get out of there and just leave those skulls where they lay," Gus ordered, already punching in a number on his cell phone.

None of them waited to be told twice.

Funny thing was, the morning didn't seem hot now. In fact Craig was downright cold, right through to his bones.

Chapter One

Sara Murdoch marked an 85 on the last history final, then dropped the red pen to the top of her desk. It clattered against the wood before rolling onto the floor and under the loaded bookshelf behind her.

She leaned back in her chair and relaxed as the feel of freedom soaked in. The spring session was over and for the first time in four years she was taking the summer session off. Just her and Kendra, roaming the mountains of northern Georgia, breathing fresh air and soaking up sunshine.

Kendra's father was supposed to have taken her for the month of June, but he'd changed those plans at the last minute, announcing that he'd be in England for the summer, getting remarried. The news had stung at first, but Sara had gotten over the pain quickly enough. Their divorce had been final for two years, and the love had died before that—if it had ever been love.

Sara wasn't at all sure she knew what love was at this point, other than the kind of love she felt for her daughter. The romantic love she'd seen in movies and read about in novels and even in history books seemed to have about the same lasting power in her life as the cotton candy Kendra loved. One sweet moment, and then it vanished, leaving nothing but that sticky saccharine aftertaste that practically gagged you.

"Are you ready to go?"

Sara scooted her chair back from her desk and motioned Raye Ann Jackson into the room. Raye Ann was chair of the history department, sweet and the most energetic sixty-something woman Sara had ever met.

"I'm ready and Kendra is so excited she's driving me nuts. She's been counting the days until we leave for two months."

"I just hope the cabin's still habitable. It's been at least four years since I've been up there. I lost the taste for it after Mark died. He always loved it so much."

"As long as it has walls and a roof, we'll make do. Roughing it will be part of the mountain experience."

"I wrote the directions down. The rural areas are a little short on road signs, but I don't think you'll have any trouble finding it. If you do, just ask anyone where Mattie's Stop is. She or Henry will be there and they can give you directions to the cabin. In fact, Mattie can tell you pretty much anything you need to know about the area. She's a nice woman, although she's a windbag. Her husband is downright strange—and grows the best vegetables I have ever put in my mouth."

"I'm sure I'll meet them."

"Oh, yes, you have to. They're as much a part of the North Georgian culture as folk music or apple cider. Here's the key and the directions," Raye Ann said, handing over a sealed white envelope. "And my phone number. If you have any questions, don't hesitate to call."

"And here's my key for you," Sara said, handing Raye Ann a key to her apartment. "Just move in whenever they start the remodeling on your house and stay as long as you need to."

"I shouldn't have to be out of the house more than a couple of weeks, but it will be nice to have somewhere to stay other than a hotel. You're sweet to share it with me."

"I'm glad it worked out so well for both of us."

"Just don't expect much from the cabin. It's rustic and the appliances were old when Mark and I bought the place twenty years ago. But there's a mountain stream that runs right by it, and the whole Chattahoochee National Forest out the back door."

"It sounds exactly like what Kendra and I need."

"Then I'll let you get back to work so you can finish up and start your summer adventure."

Sara stood and gave Raye Ann a brief hug. They didn't really see each other away from the college, didn't talk much about personal matters, but they were close in the way colleagues become when they work together for four years.

And as soon as Sara had mentioned taking the summer off and spending some time in the Appalachian Mountains in North Georgia, Raye Ann had volunteered the cabin. In fact she'd seemed delighted that the place would be used again.

As she gathered her things to leave, Sara picked up the test papers that still needed to be entered into the school's computer system and the stack of mail that had come in the morning delivery. Mostly junk from the looks of it.

An envelope slipped from her fingers as she was stuffing the mail into her canvas briefcase. It was small, like a thank-you card or an invitation. It was addressed to her, but there was no return address. Curious, she put the test papers back on the desk, picked up her chrome-handled letter opener and slit the envelope. The note inside was typed on white card stock.

Let the past stay silent.

That was it. One brief statement. No signature.

She dropped the note into the trash, then picked it up again as nebulous dread seemed to settle in the pit of her stomach. The past. What past? Her five years of marriage to Steven? The years she'd struggled working nights to put herself through college? The years she'd lied about her age and took any job she could find on the streets of Atlanta just to keep her abdomen from sinking to her backbone?

Or the five long years she'd lived in the Meyers Bickham Children's Home? Even now she got the creeps just thinking about that place. Frankly, her past sucked. So yeah, she'd let it stay silent.

Actually, she'd love for it to stay silent. And mostly it did—except when the nightmares came and the ghost baby's cry echoed in her mind like some haunting song that wouldn't stop.

This time she stuffed the note in a side pocket of her handbag, but she wasn't going to let it get to her. By tomorrow afternoon she'd be in the mountain cabin. It was going to be a great summer. And just maybe it would be so terrific that the ghost baby would finally stop crying for good.

"ARE WE ALMOST THERE, Mommy?"

It seemed like the hundredth time Kendra had asked since they left the city limits of Columbus a little over three hours ago. "Just a few more minutes, sweetie."

That was, if she could find the cutoff road. She'd followed Raye Ann's directions exactly. She'd driven through Dahlonega and was heading west on Highway 52, toward Amicolola Falls State Park. Only there was nothing to the right marked Delringer Road.

"I want to climb a mountain."

"We will, but not tonight."

"We'll have to watch out for snakes."

"We'll be very careful."

"And mosquitoes. I hate mosquitoes."

"We'll use mosquito repellent."

"Can I have a cookie?"

"Not now. It's almost dinnertime." Which would likely be peanut butter and jelly sandwiches and milk. That was about all she had with her besides fruit and cookies. She'd planned to buy groceries after they settled in the cabin, but nix that plan. Driving around at dusk looking for a seemingly nonexistent dirt road was grating enough. She wasn't about to go looking for a grocery once she'd found the cabin— if she found the cabin.

The plan had been to be there long before dark and settle in while there was still daylight. But she'd had a call from the dean at the last minute about a student protesting his grade. She'd had to stick around for a meeting to explain to the student and his parents why he couldn't skip half the classes, get failing test grades up until the final, then make a low C and expect to pass her course.

Sara drove another mile, taking the curving, mountainous highway slowly, searching for Delringer Road. *When all else fails, ask directions.* And she would, except that she was in the middle of nowhere and there wasn't a house in sight.

She was about to pull onto the shoulder and make a U-turn when she spotted the small convenience store and vegetable stand just ahead. Mattie's Stop. All right. Windbag or not, she loved the woman already. Now just let the place be open.

There was a mud-splattered black pickup truck parked in front and a sleek Harley motorcycle. So far so good. Or maybe not so good. She spotted two men standing in the shadows by the outdoor vegetable stand. One of them had on overalls over a muscle shirt, a kind of tough-guy farmer look, and even in the growing dusk, she could see the tattoos that rode his muscular biceps.

The other had on jeans and a sport shirt with the sleeves rolled up to just below his elbows. No tattoos, but he had thick, brown beard and long, scraggly hair that fell into his face.

"I don't want to buy groceries," Kendra protested, as Sara killed the engine. "I want to go to the cabin."

"We're only stopping for a minute."

"Do I have to get out?"

"Yes, you do." Sara stretched her long legs and climbed from beneath the wheel. "You can help me choose something for dinner."

"Chicken nuggets. And fries."

"You had that for lunch."

"I like chicken nuggets."

"And I like vegetables." Sara licked her lips and made a slurping noise as she loosened the belt of Kendra's booster seat. She glanced at the men once more as she moved back to let her energetic daughter jump to the cracked and uneven asphalt of the parking lot. The bearded guy was staring at her. She turned away quickly, feeling a rush of apprehension.

Kendra ran ahead of her, her red curls bouncing about her head. Her hair was even brighter than Sara's. She had Sara's freckles, too, but just a sprinkling over her nose. And there the similarity ended. Fortunately, Kendra had inherited her father's good looks.

Sara straightened her yellow cotton shirt, which had gotten scrunched beneath the seat belt, as she stepped inside the shop. Kendra was already engaged in an animated conversation with a middle-age woman with thin, frizzy brown hair and a welcoming smile.

"Your daughter says you're here for the summer."

"Yes, we're staying in a cabin on Delringer Road. That is, if I ever find it."

"You're practically there. The road's back toward Dahlonega, 'bout a mile I'd say."

"Then I missed it."

"Sign's probably down. Usually is. Don't really need it with the bridge washed out."

The last shred of Sara's optimism fell flat. "The bridge is out? What does that mean?"

"Means you can't take your vehicle past the stream. Not that there's any real reason to since that tornado two summers ago took out all the cabins up that far except the Jackson's, and they haven't been around in years. I heard Mr. Jackson died. He was such a nice man. His wife, too. Summers don't seem the same without them.''

"You must be Mattie."

"Sure am. Mattie Callahan. How'd you know?"

"Raye Ann Jackson told me about you. We're supposed to be spending the summer in her cabin. Is there another way to reach it?"

"No. Just one road. But the cabin's just on the other side of the stream. You better hurry on up there if you plan to make it tonight, though. Might be hard to find in the dark."

"What good would that do me if I can't get across the stream?"

"There's a footbridge."

Sara turned toward the sound of the voice. The bearded mountain man she'd seen outside was standing a foot behind her, though she hadn't heard him walk up. He was looking at her, his stare so intense it seemed to transcend the boundaries of space and matter and actually burrow beneath her flesh.

Kendra had been perusing the candy counter, but she left it and came over to check out the stranger. Never afraid of anything, she sidled up beside him. "Can I feel your beard?"

Sara grabbed Kendra's hand. "Don't bother the man, Kendra."

"It's all right," the man said.

He stooped and Kendra reached over and trailed her fingers through the thick, matted hair. "It feels funny."

"It's just hair."

"Did it used to be whiskers?"

"Yeah."

"My dad shaves his off."

"Most people do." He straightened and stepped past Kendra. "I took a couple of baskets of tomatoes and one each of bell peppers and squash," he said, addressing his comments to Mattie.

"No problem, Nat. I'll put them on your tab. And you might want to say howdy to these folks. They're your neighbors for the summer—staying at the Jackson cabin."

So the archetypical mountain man was her neighbor. Her *only* neighbor. Why did that not make her feel better? Still she stuck out a hand. "I'm Sara Murdoch, and this is Kendra."

He ignored her hand and the introduction, just stood there and stared at her with a look that raised the hair on the back of her neck.

"Nat," the man said, then turned and walked out of the store.

"Not much of a talker, is he," Sara said.

"Not much. His last name is Sanderson. Nat lives alone and minds his own business. Grows terrific apples, though. He talks more to Henry than anyone else. And I reckon he talks to that boy from Dahlonega he's got working for him."

"Henry?"

"My husband. You probably saw him when you came in. Big guy. Folks around her call him Junk Yard Dog, 'cause ain't nobody gonna' mess with him. Except me, of course. And our daughter Dorinda. She has him wrapped around her little finger. You'll meet her while you're here. She's goes to school down at University of Georgia, but she's home for the summer. Gonna be a teacher."

Sara waited until Mattie stopped for breath before she broke in. "I need to get to the cabin, but I'll take a basket of the tomatoes and peppers I saw outside and I need to pick up a few things for dinner tonight and breakfast in the morning."

"Certainly, honey, you just go right ahead. If you need any help finding what you need, I'll be over here sweeping up. I like the place clean when I leave at night. We open at ten in the morning, and…"

Sara turned and scanned the small store for Kendra. She was at the candy rack, a pack of M&M's already in hand and reaching for some gummy bears.

"You can choose one treat," Sara said, this time not waiting for Mattie to stop for air, which didn't seem to bother Mattie. She went right on talking until she finished what she had to say.

"Can I get two? I'll save one for tomorrow."

"One—for after dinner."

"Yes, ma'am," Kendra said, rolling her eyes.

The store was small, a wooden shell about twelve by eighteen, but it seemed to have the essentials. Milk, bread, eggs, cheese, luncheon meat and a few condiments for sandwiches.

Sara shopped quickly, eager to reach the cabin while there was still enough daylight to find it. "Anything else I should know?" Sara asked as Mattie rang up her purchases.

"Not that I can think of. Just be careful. Keep a close eye on your daughter out in those woods. You don't want her to get lost."

"I will."

"I'll help you get these to your car," Mattie offered.

"That's okay. I think I can handle them." Sara

picked up the bags of groceries, giving the one with just a loaf of bread to Kendra.

"Don't forget to grab a basket of those tomatoes and peppers on your way out. Once you taste them, you'll be back for more."

"I'm sure I'll be back often."

"Good. We're neighbors. Drop in any time, even if it's just to chat or ask questions."

"Thanks."

Sara hesitated at the door. Both the truck and the motorcycle were still parked outside. Nat was leaning against the cycle and Henry's hand was on the door of the truck.

She deposited the groceries in the car, then took Kendra's hand when she walked over to the vegetable stand to get the produce.

Henry followed her there. "You folks staying around here somewhere?"

"At the Jackson cabin."

"That place still standing?"

"I hope so."

"You ever been there before?"

"No."

"Well, don't be expecting to find much when you get there."

"I'm not."

Nat started the motorcycle, practically drowning out their conversation. Henry turned and waved for him to kill the engine. When he did, Henry took a step in his direction. "You ought to show these two young ladies up to the Jackson cabin, Nat. Make sure they find the place in the dark."

Nat stared at her without comment.

"That's not necessary," Sara said.

"Could be," Henry said. "You don't want to go hiking around in the dark looking for the place. Not with the girl, here."

True, but she wasn't sure she wanted to go hiking around in the dark woods with the scraggly recluse biker, either.

"Just follow me," Nat said.

He started the engine again and slipped the helmet over his head. *Follow him.*

"You're not worried about Nat, are you?" Henry asked.

"A little," she admitted.

"No need of that. He's a loner, but that don't make him bad. He just deals with things his way, like we all do if we want to survive. He won't talk much, but he'll make sure you and the kid get where you're going and that you're safe."

She nodded, still uneasy, but knowing there was no reason not to trust Henry. No reason not to trust Nat for that matter. She'd never been one to judge a book by its cover. She grabbed the baskets of vegetables and walked to her van then buckled Kendra into her seat and turned back toward the store. Mattie and Henry were both standing in the open doorway, smiling and waving, more assurance that there was nothing to worry about.

Sara backed out of the parking lot, following the bright red taillights of the mountain man's bike.

A mile later she turned and followed him down the unmarked dirt road. Tall pines bordered the narrow road, cutting off the last glimmer of the fading light and plunging them into the gathering darkness of the forest.

Just her and Kendra and a bearded mountain man

with the darkest eyes she'd ever seen, traveling to an isolated cabin at the end of a washed-out road.

Apprehension slithered along her nerve endings at the thought and her grip tightened on the steering wheel. But it was rural Georgia. It was safe here. She held on to that thought as full darkness set in.

Chapter Two

After fifteen minutes on a curving road banked by sheer drop-offs, they arrived at the literal end of the road, a downed tree someone had stretched across the road to keep unknowing drivers from plunging into the stream.

Nat pulled off the road and veered to the right, parking so that his headlights illuminated an overgrown path through the woods. Sara pulled her beige van in beside the motorbike and left her lights on as well. There was no cabin in sight. No footbridge, either. Just her and Kendra and a bearded stranger who didn't care much for talking.

Her anxiety level shot skyward and she considered jerking the van into reverse and speeding away. Instead she left the motor running and lowered the window. "I don't see a cabin."

"It's hidden in the trees. But the footbridge is only a few yards away, just down that path—or what's left of the path. I think we should take a look at the place before you start unloading."

"Good idea." The guy had made a couple of complete sentences. That had to be a good sign. Besides, he seemed to know what he was talking about. That eased her probably irrational fears enough that she climbed out of the car.

"Are we there, Mommy?"

"Close." She helped Kendra from her car seat as Nat grabbed a flashlight from a leather bag on the back of his bike. She reached back into her glove compartment and took out her flashlight as well. A nice heavy one.

If this guy tried anything, she'd crack his skull with it, then give him a quick, hard kick to the groin, a trick she'd learned during her first year of living on the streets.

"I'll carry the girl if that's okay," Nat said. "It's pretty tricky walking through the undergrowth if you're not used to it."

Sara would have preferred carrying Kendra herself, but not only were there vines and weeds in the path, there were branches to dodge. It was pretty much all she could do to maneuver through the brush herself. Something rustled in the grass underfoot, and she jumped in the air then tripped on a large pointed rock, catching herself on an overhanging limb before she fell on her face.

"You all right?"

"Oh, yeah. I'm just great."

Nat kept walking with Kendra perched atop his broad shoulders. He kept a steady pace, though he walked with a noticeable limp in his right leg.

"Isn't this fun, Mommy?" Kendra said, giggling and holding on tight to Nat's neck. "We're having an adventure."

"You bet," Sara agreed as a prickly bush ripped a strip of skin from her leg. "Really fun!"

Kendra kept up a barrage of questions. Nat came

up with a few answers, albeit short ones. It was probably more than the guy had talked in months. Sara just concentrated on where she was putting her feet, avoiding rocks and hopefully the snakes that she imagined slithering under the grass.

"There it is," Nat said.

The first thing Sara saw was the footbridge, or at least what was left of it. It was basically a few planks of wood nailed together. Half-rotted wood with gaping holes big enough to fall through if you made a misstep.

"Is that thing safe?"

Nat took Kendra from his shoulders and set her on the ground next to Sara. "I'll check it out." He stepped gingerly on the bridge, then walked slowly to the other side, giving the railings a few solid shakes.

"It's not safe, but it's crossable."

That's when Sara noticed the cabin, a few yards from the bridge but in full view. She breathed a sigh of relief. It really did exist and her rugged mountain man really had delivered them to it. The cabin looked pretty much as Raye Ann had described it. Rustic, sheltered by towering pines, with a roof that hung over the porch and a slatted swing that creaked in the slight breeze.

"A house in the woods, just like the three bears," Kendra squealed. She tried to tug from Sara's grasp.

"You have to hold my hand crossing the bridge," Sara said firmly. "And don't pull or try to run."

Nat waited for them. Once they were across the bridge, Kendra dropped Sara's hand and grabbed his. "Are you going to stay with us?" she asked.

"No. Mr. Nat just came along to help us find the cabin," Sara said, answering for him.

With her usual boundless energy, Kendra skipped ahead of both Sara and Nat and ran up the three slightly lopsided steps and gave the porch swing a big push before running to the front door.

Nat stood back while Sara unlocked the door and shoved it open. A silky spiderweb brushed across her face and stuck to her eyelashes as she searched the wall for a light switch. Her fingers found and clicked the switch and the overhead fixture spread a dim glow over the room.

"It looks like Halloween," Kendra announced, dashing inside and making a hand print in the layers of dust that coated a small table.

Halloween was an apt description, especially with the abundance of spiderwebs and the strange dead bug that lay smack-dab in the middle of the floor. Sara groaned.

"Not very welcoming," Nat said.

The understatement of the day. Sara kicked the bug out of the way and surveyed the room. Once you got past the first impression, it wasn't so bad. Pine floors that needed a good mopping. A stone fireplace flanked by redwood rockers and an upholstered sofa, brown and thankfully covered in protective plastic. And built-in shelves across the back of the room, all filled with old photographs, dusty game boxes and well-worn books.

"It has a certain charm," Sara said, determined to make the best of the situation. "A little elbow grease and lots of cleanser and it will be fine."

"Are you sure? They have places up at the state park you can rent."

"We expected rustic. The cabin will do."

"It's your call. If you're staying, I may as well start hauling in your things."

Now that surprised her. She'd expected him to cut out the second she said she was staying. But she could really use some help with the heavier items, especially when crossing that rickety bridge.

Nat pushed through the front door. "You stay right here," she told Kendra. "Sit in that rocking chair and don't move while I help Mr. Nat bring in our gear."

"Easier if I do it by myself," Nat said. He stalked away without waiting for a response.

Sara sighed. A strange man, but helpful.

"Will you play checkers with me?" Kendra asked, already pulling a box from the shelf. The top shifted and several of the black and red disks clattered to the floor, rolling away in all directions.

"Games later. Let's check out the rest of the cabin now. We have to find your bedroom."

The remainder of the checkers fell from the box as Kendra tried to set it back on the shelf. Sara helped her pick them up, hurriedly so that Nat wouldn't step on one and slip with the luggage. Even reclusive mountain guys probably knew about lawsuits.

She started her tour by opening and peeking through the four doors that opened off of the living area. And that was pretty much all there was to see. The cabin was basically a square broken into four rooms, without a hallway.

Prompted by a few hunger pains, she checked out the kitchen first. Stepping to the gas range, she ran her hand along the black grates. They were covered in dust, but not greasy. Apparently the place had been left clean. "Guess we can eat, Kendra. We have a kitchen for cooking."

"Aww. I'd rather have McDonald's."

"Atta girl. But not tonight." No way would she try to find this place again in the dark, not until she knew her way around a lot better than she did now.

Kendra ducked under her arm as she opened the refrigerator, saw it was empty, then scooted away. It was also hot. Sara got down on all fours, found the loose electrical connection and plugged it in. A nice humming sound vibrated from the aged refrigerator. Hopefully that meant the thing was going to cool.

"Stay inside," Sara cautioned as she heard the front screen door squeak open.

"Why can't I go on the porch and swing?"

"There are mosquitoes and I haven't unpacked the repellent."

Sara finished her inspection of the refrigerator, grimacing when she saw plastic ice-cube trays instead of an ice maker. She hadn't even known they made those nuisances anymore. But on the bright side, she loved the kitchen table. Solid oak with big claw-footed legs. And it sat right in front of a window with a view of the mountains.

There was a large cupboard on the back wall. Instead of doors, it was fronted with a gingham curtain. One more thing that needed washing. The only contents were a box of ice cream salt and a fire extinguisher—and a partially decomposed wasp.

But the cabinet over the tiled counter was full of dishes. Melamine. They'd definitely been around for a while. And there were glasses, stainless steel tableware and an assortment of pots and pans. Everything she and Kendra would need for the summer. And at a price she could afford. Free.

The bedrooms were equally as sparse. Twin beds in one, a full-size bed in the other, a four-drawer chest and a tiny closet in each. All the beds were covered in chenille spreads that had probably once been white but were now faded to a dull yellow and liberally sprinkled with dust and pollen.

Kendra rejoined her, holding a book about edible berries that she'd apparently found on the bookshelf. She hopped up on the twin bed that occupied the space below a narrow window. "I'll sleep here, so I can see the stars."

"Good idea. I'll put your Little Mermaid sheets and your yellow blanket on the bed, and you'll feel right at home."

"Where's the bathroom?"

A bathroom. Surely there was one, but she didn't remember seeing it.

"It's behind the kitchen."

Sara looked around to find Nat standing in the doorway holding a large suitcase in each hand. The muscles in his arms strained against the cotton fabric of his plaid shirt and his long hair fell across his forehead, skimming the top of his brows.

"How do you know that?" she asked.

"I've checked the place out before. I figured it was deserted since I've never seen anyone around."

"How could you check it out? It was locked."

"The door was locked. The windows weren't. They don't even have latches. Not a lot of use for locks when you're the only one around for miles."

Nat stepped closer. He dwarfed the room and all of a sudden the apprehension hit again. Only the sensations jumping along her nerve endings didn't really feel like fear. She wasn't sure what they felt like, just that her insides were shaky and she was having difficulty swallowing.

"Where do you want these?" Nat asked, nodding toward the luggage he was holding.

"The green one goes in here," she said, managing to keep her voice steady. "The black one goes in the other bedroom."

He set the green suitcase on the other twin bed, then turned and walked away. Sara took a deep breath and tried to put the situation into a reasonable perspective. It couldn't be attraction. Not to someone whose face she could barely see beneath the hair and whose eyes seemed to look right through her.

"I'm going to help the man with the beard."

"No." The word came out too quickly and far too forcefully.

"But he has a hurt leg, Mommy. He shouldn't have to do all the work himself."

"I want you to stay inside."

Kendra jumped from the bed, propped her hands on her hips and stuck out her bottom lip. "Why? There's nothing scary about the dark. You tell me that every time I have a bad dream."

"You're not big enough to carry heavy things."

"I can carry my toys and my bag of movies."

"You might fall into the water."

"I won't fall. I'm a big girl."

"I think Mr. Nat would prefer we stay out of his way. But you could help me by unpacking your suitcase. You can decide which drawer to use for your pajamas, which one to use for your underwear and socks and which one is best for your play clothes."

"And I can put my shoes in the closet."

"Good girl." Sara pulled her close and gave her a quick hug. "But first let's go check out that bathroom."

Sara flushed the toilet, then breathed a sigh of relief as the brownish water twirled and drained and some yellowish metal-stained water replaced it. It didn't look great, but it worked. That would do for now. By the time Sara returned to the living room, Nat was bringing in yet another load, the 13-inch VCR/TV in his right hand, a five gallon bottle of drinking water in the crook of his left arm.

"You can't get any decent TV coverage up here without a dish," he said, setting the TV on the floor.

"It's for Disney movies. Kendra's addicted to them."

"Do you want me to set it in the girl's room?"

"You can just leave it there for now. In fact, you can just stack everything else on the floor in here as well. I'll sift through it later and put it away once I've finished cleaning."

He nodded and his gaze lingered on her. She was hit again by his mesmerizing eyes. Dark. Brooding. Unreadable.

"How old is your daughter?"

"She'll be five next week."

"Watch her around the water. The creek's low now but it can come up fast after a rain."

"I'll do that."

"And don't let her wander into the woods alone. It would be easy to get lost out there."

He didn't say more, just turned and walked away, but his concern for her daughter surprised Sara. She hadn't expected it of him, but then when she'd first seen him she wouldn't have expected he'd be here unloading her gear tonight, either.

Still, something about him made her uneasy, and she didn't need that, not tucked away in the middle of the woods with no neighbors except him for miles around.

Not that it mattered. She doubted she'd see him again unless she ran into him at Mattie's. It was just her, Kendra and the spiders. But, hey, the toilet flushed and the refrigerator hummed. And there were no lectures to give or test papers to grade. What more could a woman need?

SARA WOKE to a stream of sunlight that forced its way through the dirt-streaked windows and highlighted a chorus line of dancing dust specks. She stretched, thought of the cabin cleaning chores waiting for her and threw her legs over the side of the bed.

She'd slept amazingly well, waking only once. Then she'd had a brief moment of dread, had wondered if she'd made a mistake in coming to such an isolated place for the summer. But when she'd glanced out the window and seen the heavens full of sparkling stars winking at her, her fears had dissolved.

Sara started to pull on her robe, then decided against it. There was no one to see or care if she had her morning coffee outside in her pajamas. Padding across the bare wood floors, she went to the kitchen and started the brewing process in the automatic drip pot she'd brought from home. She could rough it to a point, but her coffee had to be right.

A few minutes later, cup of java in hand, Sara

walked outside and plopped onto the porch swing. A cool breeze brushed her face and a crow cawed at her from the lower branches of a hickory tree. The sights, the sounds, even the smells were familiar.

The mountains had been the nicest part of her life at Meyers Bickham—actually the only good part. She'd escaped there every chance she'd gotten, wandered as far away from the old church-turned-orphanage as she dared. It was never far enough.

The note she'd received two days ago crept into her mind. *Let the past stay silent.* She still had no idea who'd sent it or why. If it was a threat, it hadn't been very clear. Not that it mattered. She had no intention of talking or even thinking about the past, starting right now. It was much too beautiful a day to deal with depressing thoughts.

She'd tackle a few of the cleaning chores, then go into Dahlonega for a bigger selection of groceries and some pamphlets on things to do in the area that Kendra might enjoy. She might even stop by and chat with Mattie. It would be nice to find out a bit more about her only neighbor. Not that she was really interested or that she expected to see him again. But the guy was weird and something about him did make her insides a little shaky.

She'd like to know the story behind those dark, brooding eyes. And to make sure she had nothing to worry about.

SARA CHOSE a bag of wheat sandwich rolls from the bread display while Mattie was ringing up the purchases of a middle-aged couple. She didn't want to ask about Nat in front of anyone, not even Kendra, who was standing a few feet away, eyeing the candy shelf.

When the couple left, Sara stepped to the counter.

"How's the cabin?" Mattie asked.

"It was dusty and decorated with cobwebs and dead insects, but it's shaping up."

"Glad to hear it. Did you try those tomatoes?"

"I sliced one for a sandwich last night. It was delicious."

"Nothing beats homegrown and vine-ripened tomatoes. Henry picked the ones that are out there now just this morning."

"Then I'll have to get another basket."

"Sure thing. What else do you need today?"

Sara turned to make certain Kendra was still in sight but not close enough to listen in on the conversation. Never one to stay in one place long, her daughter had moved to the souvenir section and was watching the simulated snow fall in a small glass globe.

"I have a couple of questions," Sara said, keeping her voice low.

"Shoot. I've lived here all my life. If I don't know the answers, they're probably not worth having." Mattie laughed, and the deep wrinkles around her eyes intensified.

"I was wondering about Nat Sanderson."

"Most people do. He's a strange one. Pretty much a recluse. Henry said he was going to show you to the cabin last night. That surprised me, but I guess Henry probably pushed him into it. The guy just don't have much to do with anybody 'cept Henry and me, and we only see him when he comes around the store."

"He's okay, though, isn't he?"

"Harmless, you mean?"

"Right."

"Seems harmless to me. Don't do nothing but work in that apple orchard of his, mostly by himself. Grows the best apples in the county, though. All organic. People come from clear down in Atlanta to stock up on them come fall."

"How long has he lived here?"

"Showed up about three years ago. Bought the Delringers' old place. Orchard and house had pretty much gone to rot since old man Delringer died. Surprised us that anyone bought it. And that's about all any of us know about Nat, though there's lots of speculation."

"What kind of speculation?"

"Some folks think he's on the run from the law and that Nat's not his real name. Just an alias, you know?"

"Why do they think that?"

"Some of 'em just like to talk to hear their tongues rattle. Others don't have nothing better to do than sit around making up stories about anyone who's different or who don't talk to them when they try to start a conversation."

"What do you think of him?"

"Don't rightly know. I sell his apples and cider for him and he gives me a generous cut. It's a good deal for both of us. I usually owe him money. He gets his vegetables from me. We settle up at the end of every month."

A car pulled up in front of the store and an attractive woman who looked to be in her early twenties got out. Kendra met her at the door. She never considered anyone a stranger. Sara couldn't be too careful about keeping on eye on her.

"Then you think all the negative speculation about Nat Sanderson is unfounded?"

Mattie frowned. "I haven't had no trouble with him and Henry likes him. But then Henry's kind of a quiet one, too, especially sometimes when he gets to thinking about 'Nam." Mattie looked up at the newest arrival and a big smile split her lips. "Come on over here, Dorinda. Let me introduce you to the woman that's staying in the Jackson cabin."

They went through the introductions. Dorinda and Kendra got to know each other better while Sara paid for her purchases.

Mattie leaned across the counter when she gave Sara her change, keeping her voice low. "I think Nat's just a man who's seen some suffering. Take that for what it's worth. I ain't no psychiatrist, but I'm usually a darn good judge of people."

Mattie patted Sara's hand as if they were old friends, then walked over to where Kendra was helping Dorinda fill the cooler with cans of soft drinks, a task Mattie had apparently started and not finished.

"If you ever need a baby-sitter while you're up here, I'm usually available," Dorinda said.

"Yeah, Mommy, can I go to her house?"

"Not today, but I'll definitely keep that in mind."

"Anytime. If I don't have anything to do, my dad will have me out cutting okra or picking peas or else I'll be here minding the store. I'll take baby-sitting over those any day."

Dorinda walked to the van with them and buckled Kendra into her booster seat. "Is this your first time in this area?" she asked.

"My first time in the immediate area," Sara said. "I grew up west of here."

"There's lots to do. You should visit Helen. It's been made to look like an Alpine village. And the state park has nature activities for children every week. I always volunteer some when I'm home from school."

"Thanks. And I'll keep you in mind about that baby-sitting. I plan to spend most of my time with Kendra, but you never know when I might need a break."

"Just call me. I can come to your place, or you can bring her to the farm. You'd never know it to look at him, but Daddy loves having kids around. He'll let her feed the chickens and geese and show her the new colts."

"In that case, I'll definitely have to let her visit."

Sara was glad she'd stopped in and asked her questions, and glad she'd met Dorinda. She reminded Sara of some of her brighter and more motivated students.

But Sara still didn't have a handle on Nat Sanderson. Some thought he was running from the law. Mattie thought he was a man who'd suffered. And all Sara knew was that she felt strange when he was around, as if she were coming down with a virus.

Hopefully she wouldn't have to give it another thought. If he was the loner Mattie said, she'd never see the man again.

SARA BALANCED a bag of groceries on her hip while she locked the door of the van. Maneuvering the path hadn't been nearly as difficult in the daylight, but it was still overgrown and had enough vines and invading branches to make walking feel like a trek on *Survivor*. And the footbridge would be a major challenge with Kendra and groceries to manage.

She took Kendra's hand, then stopped dead still at the sound of footfalls coming through the woods.

And there he was. Nat Sanderson, all six plus feet of him, sweaty, his hair falling into his face, his boots caked with mud, his eyes cool and dark as night.

And a scythe clutched in his right hand. Every woman's incubus. Only, Sara was wide awake.

Chapter Three

It was like a scene straight from a horror movie—only Nat was staring at her questioningly with those brooding eyes. She pulled Kendra close. "What are you doing here?" she demanded.

Nat stopped and stared at her. "I'm clearing the path so that you don't have to fight your way to the house. What did you think I was doing?"

"I don't know. You frightened me. I don't like it when someone sneaks up on me."

"I don't sneak. I came out to clear the path and rebuild your footbridge before it collapses, but I'll leave if you want."

"He didn't scare me, Mommy. He's our friend."

Kendra tugged from her grasp and went to stand by Nat. "What's that?" she said, pointing to the scythe.

"It's a tool to cut low bushes and high grass, and it's very sharp, so children should never touch it." He tossed it over in the grass away from the path and turned his gaze back to Sara. "Let me get this straight. Were you frightened because you were startled, or are you afraid of me?"

She exhaled sharply, not knowing if she was more

upset with Nat or herself, but wanting to be reasonably honest. "It's not as if I actually know you. We met last night at a vegetable stand alongside the highway."

"And I could have left you to find your own way up here in the dark. Could have let you unload your own gear. And I sure don't have to be here now, so if my having long hair and a beard makes you uncomfortable, I'll just cut out now."

Blunt and to the point. She may as well be, too. "You take some getting used to. And I have a tendency to overreact."

"So do you want me to finish what I came for or not?"

"I'd appreciate your help, if we can go back to being civil."

"I'm not big on social graces."

"I've noticed." She turned and scanned the area. "Did you walk out here? I don't see your bike."

"Can't carry a lot of lumber on my bike. I borrowed Blake's truck."

"Who's Blake?"

"A young guy from Dahlonega who helps me out some in the orchard."

"So where's Blake's truck?"

"I took the old logging road over. It comes out behind the cabin."

"So why didn't you bring me that way last night?"

"I doubt your van would have made it. It's half washed out and full of potholes. And not a place you'd want to get stuck."

"No. Delringer Road is adventuresome enough for me."

''I'll need to use the electrical outlets in the cabin to run my power saw, but don't worry, I'll do the cutting outside. Blake keeps a heavy duty extension cord in his truck tool box.''

''Good. That's the one thing other than the kitchen sink that I didn't bring with me.''

''No kitchen sink? I was almost certain I unloaded one of those last night.''

His lips split into a hint of a smile. The change made him look younger—and less the frightening, reclusive mountain man who had just scared her out of her senses. He had good teeth. Very white and straight. Not what you'd expect from a man who didn't shave or get haircuts.

Now that she thought about it, his clothes didn't fit with the scraggly hair and beard, either. His jeans were faded but clean, and his plaid cotton shirt had a crease in the sleeve. It had been ironed.

''I'll be around the rest of the day if you need anything,'' she said as she took Kendra's hand again and started down the path. It had been cleared to the point that walking it wasn't a risky venture of avoiding things that slithered through the high grass and tree limbs that endeavored to punch your eyes out.

''I like Mr. Nat, Mommy. He cut our weeds.''

Which beat the hell out of cutting their throats, the scenario that had run through her mind a few minutes ago. She felt ridiculous for even thinking it now, but still there was something about the man that didn't add up. And things that didn't add up made her nervous.

NAT LIKED the steady rhythm and the pull on his muscles as he tapped nail after nail into the planks, reinforcing the footbridge with the lumber. The work was satisfying and easy. It was the overpowering need to come back here today that bothered him.

For three years he'd managed to avoid almost all involvement with the natives and the tourists. Except for Henry and Mattie, he'd hardly talked to anyone other than the hellos and thank-yous that were mandatory when you lived in Georgia. Well, he talked to Blake, of course, but that was mostly to tell his part-time helper what needed to be done in the orchard.

Now here he was, doing chores for a spunky red-head who was living practically under his nose for the entire summer. Not that he had a lot of choice. That old footbridge was going to collapse any day now. And if they'd fallen in and gotten hurt, or maybe even drowned if the water was up, he'd have had to tote the guilt for that on top of the load he already carried.

He muttered a string of curses under his breath as the memories ran rampant in his mind. Time was supposed to be the great healer, but it had been three and a half years, and he still couldn't think about all that had happened that last night in D.C., without feeling as if someone were tightening a vise grip on his heart.

He sat down on the bridge and let his legs dangle over the sides, but his gaze was drawn to the cabin. Kendra was lying on the porch, coloring a picture on a large square of white paper. One of the few times he'd seen her so quiet.

Sara was stretching to sweep cobwebs down from the corners along the porch roof. He liked the way she moved, easy, natural, her braless breasts jiggling beneath the white T-shirt. If she wore any makeup at all, he couldn't see it. But her cheeks were tinged in pink like the apples when they first started to turn. Her hair was wild, loose locks shooting out everywhere from the ponytail that bounced behind her when she walked.

Kendra stood and jumped down the porch steps one at a time, like a two-footed rabbit. She waved at him and came bounding in his direction. "I like the new bridge, Mr. Nat."

"Thanks."

"I can help you finish it."

Her standing there made him nervous, but he couldn't very well tell her to vamoose. "Do you want to hammer a nail into one of the boards?"

"Sure. I'm good at hammering."

"Have you hammered before?"

"No, but I'll still be good at it."

Just like a woman. He handed her the hammer. "You gotta be careful with it."

"It's heavy," she said, holding it with two hands.

Everything felt heavy right now. Nat should just get up and leave, come back and finish this when Sara and Kendra were away. He didn't. Maybe the years had gotten him somewhere after all. Or maybe he was just a glutton for punishment.

SARA WATCHED as Nat stooped down beside Kendra and helped her hammer a nail into the wood. Kids and dogs were supposed to be the best judge of a person's character, but Sara wasn't ready to fully trust that old adage. That had to be why she was so aware of his presence.

She finished the last stretch of porch roof just as

her cell phone rang. She raced into the house and grabbed it. "Hello."

"How's life in the little cabin in the big woods?" Raye Ann asked in her delightful Georgia drawl.

"Full of cobwebs and dirt," Sara answered, walking back to the porch.

"Don't say I didn't warn you. The spiders love that place, as does every other kind of bug in existence. Have you met any of the neighbors?"

"Actually there's only one neighbor." Sara explained about the bridge being washed out and not being replaced because the cabins farther up the mountain had been lost to a tornado. "I've met the one neighbor, though. A bearded recluse who grows apples organically."

"He must have bought the Delringers' old orchard."

"Three years ago. And I met Mattie and Henry from Mattie's Stop, and their daughter, Dorinda."

"Dorinda must be in college by now."

"The University of Georgia. She's studying to be a teacher."

"Good for her. So is the cabin livable?"

"It's getting there. I have all the doors and windows open today, airing the place out. Now I'm into serious spiderweb removal."

"Better you than me, but I didn't actually call just to chat."

"Don't tell me the dean wants me to come back and meet with another complaining student."

"No, it's actually about that old orphanage where you were raised—Meyers Bickham."

The warning note that she'd all but forgotten flew

into her mind, carrying with it a rush of apprehension. ''What about Meyers Bickham?''

''They're tearing it down.''

''It's probably falling down. It practically was when I was there and it's been closed for years.''

''No. There's a demolition crew there and they found the remains of what appears to be infants in the walls of the basement. It was the top story on the noon news today. They said there would be a full investigation.''

Babies buried in the basement walls. It was horribly creepy. Like a nightmare that burst into life in the light of day.

''Are you okay?'' Raye Ann asked. ''I didn't mean to upset you. I just thought you might find that interesting and I know how easy it is to miss out on the news altogether when you're up at the cabin.''

''I'm okay, though it does sound gruesome. And you're right. I hadn't heard.''

''Oh, and one other thing. The department secretary said that someone from a historical society in Savannah called yesterday to talk to you about giving a talk. She told them you were spending the summer at my cabin in the mountains but gave them your cell phone number. They said they probably would wait until you were back on campus, but I thought I'd let you know in case you were interested in setting something up with them while you're off.''

''Thanks, but I'm sure I'll put it off until fall even if they call. I'm in my shorts and T-shirt mode now, and the thought of tugging on a pair of panty hose sounds like torture.''

''Ah, yes, I remember those summers well.''

''You can join us.''

"I'd think about it if I didn't need to be here while they remodel the house. I'm moving into your apartment tomorrow if that's okay. They're starting to take up the kitchen floor and my allergies will go wild with all that dust."

"Move in anytime."

They talked a minute more. They didn't mention Meyers Bickham again, but Sara couldn't shake the news of the bodies from her mind. She'd always thought the basement was haunted. And it had been. Lost souls hidden away in the damp brick.

Damn! That must be why she'd gotten that note yesterday. Someone knew the story was about to break, and whoever had written it thought that Sara knew something they didn't want told. She closed her eyes, then opened them again at Kendra's shrill call. "I'm helping make the bridge, Mommy."

"I see you are, sweetie."

"You want to come watch me?"

"I'll be there in a minute." When she'd pulled herself together enough that Kendra wouldn't see how shaken she was. Babies buried in the walls of an orphanage. It was positively depraved.

She went to the kitchen and took out her frustration on a bowl full of lemons, squeezing them in her bare hands until nothing was left but dry pulp. She made lemonade with the juice, poured it over three tall glasses of ice and carried them to the porch.

Kendra had apparently tired of pounding nails and had returned to the picture she'd been coloring earlier. "I like the colors you're using," Sara said, setting a glass of the lemonade down next to her.

"It's our cabin. The yellow is the sun and the brown is our swing. Next I'm going to draw a picture of Mr. Nat with his beard. It's longer than even Santa Claus's beard, but it's not white.''

Sara took the other two glasses and walked to the footbridge. Nat looked up as she approached, then went right back to his work.

''I brought you some lemonade,'' she said. ''I thought you might be thirsty for something besides water.''

''Lemonade's always nice.'' He hammered in the nail he was holding, then joined her on the bank of the stream. She held out the glass, but instead of taking it, he unbuttoned his shirt, used it to wipe the perspiration from his face, then tossed it over a large jagged rock at their feet.

His chest was muscled and bronzed from the sun, with a sprinkling of dark hairs that clustered around his nipples and disappeared in a V at his waist. She realized she was staring and moved her gaze to his face.

When their gazes met, she felt that same crazy intrusiveness that she'd felt last night, an intensity that seemed to bore right through her. Only this time, she felt something more, an awareness that she was standing close to a man who smelled of perspiration and musk and seemed as potent and earthy as the woods that surrounded them.

''You might not want to get too close,'' he said, stepping away from her. ''I probably smell as hot and sweaty as I feel.''

''The smell of a working man. That can't be all bad.''

He put the glass to his lips and drank, his Adam's apple jostling as he swallowed. When he'd finished half the glass, he sat down on the edge of the stream, stretched his legs in front of him and leaned back on his elbows.

"You must be tired," she said.

"No more than usual."

"You've done a great job on the bridge. You seem to have a talent for it."

"I just nailed a few boards together. There's not a lot of talent needed for that."

"Maybe not, but I couldn't have done it, at least not as well or as quickly as you have." She sat down beside him, half expecting him to move away. He didn't so she decided to keep talking. If she got to know him, it might defuse some of the edginess she felt when he was around. And talking about something other than Meyers Bickham might still some of the haunting memories Raye Ann's call had stirred. "You don't sound as if you're from Georgia."

"I'm not."

"What brought you here?"

"I was driving through the area and saw the For Sale sign on the orchard. It seemed to suit me."

"So you just bought it and started raising apples."

"It works for me."

"You don't really like to talk about yourself, do you?"

"Not particularly."

"Mattie says you're a recluse."

"I'd say that fits."

"Yet you not only helped me find the cabin and get settled in last night, you came back out here today to build us a safe footbridge. Why?"

"You looked as if you needed a little help. I'd say you still do, though I doubt it's the kind of help I can offer."

"You're very insightful for a recluse."

"Not particularly. You're shredding that napkin you're holding into tiny bits."

So she was. She wadded up the pieces and stuffed them into the pocket of her denim shorts.

"Won't be much of a vacation if you bring your problems with you," he said.

"I don't have to bring them along. I have this past that doesn't let go of me," she said, for some reason feeling a need to explain her answer.

"Pasts have a way of doing that." He finished his lemonade and stood, no doubt eager to get back to his work and out of earshot of her problems. He didn't bother with his shirt, just picked up his hammer and grabbed a plank from the pile of lumber he'd cut into carefully measured pieces. "Let it go," he said. "If there's any way you can, just let it go. If you can't do it for yourself, do it for your daughter."

His voice grew husky on the last few words, and she had the weird feeling that the conversation was more about him now than her. About him and whatever had chased him from the world he'd known before he'd moved into these mountains and holed up in a world for one.

She was considering asking him to join them for lunch when she heard a car on the washed out road.

"Sounds like company," Nat said.

"I can't imagine who it would be."

It took less than five minutes to find out. Two men, neither of whom she'd ever seen before, turned from the path and started toward the footbridge. One was tall, nice-looking, probably somewhere in his mid-forties. The other was younger, blond with a winning smile and a dimple in his left cheek. They stopped at the bridge and stood there for a second, staring at Nat who stared right back.

The older man pulled out his wallet and let it fall open to reveal an official-looking ID. "I'm Jack Trotter, FBI. And this is my partner Bruce Dagger. We're here to see Sara Murdoch."

"I'm Sara Murdoch." She glanced around to check on Kendra. She was running toward them, as always eager to check out any visitor who came to call.

"Can you tell me what this is about?" Sara said, reaching out to grab Kendra's hand.

"The Meyers Bickham Children's Home. You were a resident there, weren't you?"

Her heart raced. She'd never even gotten a speeding ticket before. Now she had FBI agents calling on her.

"We just want to ask you a few questions," Jack said. "Alone." He glanced at Nat.

Nat stood back and let them pass him on the bridge. "I can look after Kendra for you while you talk," he offered.

"That's okay. I'll take her inside with me. She can watch a movie in her bedroom. She's probably had enough sun for awhile."

Pressure swelled in Sara's temples as they walked up the stairs and into the cabin. She didn't know a thing, yet she was certain she was about to be dragged into the depravity of the babies who'd been buried in the wall.

Somewhere in the back of her mind she heard the haunting cries that had lived with her for twenty years. The sound of the ghost baby crying out to her for help. Only this time the ghost baby had apparently called in the FBI.

There was no way this could be good.

Chapter Four

Sara had never been involved in any kind of investigation, which gave the two self-assured men sitting opposite her a distinct advantage. Not to mention that they were dressed meticulously and she had on her faded denim cutoffs, a T-shirt that bore the emblem of the college where she taught and a pair of mud-stained tennis shoes.

"You're not easy to find, Mrs. Murdoch."

"How *did* you find me?"

"The Bureau has its ways."

"Then I'm surprised you didn't also learn that I don't know anything about the remains of infants that were found in the basement walls at Meyers Bickham."

"Sometimes people know more than they think they do." Jack Trotter leaned back against the sofa cushions and crossed his right ankle over his left knee, as if they were having a friendly discussion. So far he had done all the talking, while the younger guy seemed more intent on looking out the front window.

Finally Bruce nodded and turned his attention to

her. "You lived at Meyers Bickham what? Five years? Ten years?"

"Five years."

She thought of the phone call Raye Ann had mentioned, and wondered if the "historical society" had been the FBI's ruse to find her.

"You must have seen and heard a lot in five years."

"I did. I heard rules and lectures and work schedules. I saw children degraded, supervisors lose their tempers and I washed enough dirty dishes and cleaned enough bathrooms to last a lifetime."

"But no bodies?"

"Never. No one ever died while I was there, at least not that I know of. Kids left all the time to go into foster homes or because they were adopted, but no one died. The bodies must have been there from when it was used as a church."

"Could have been."

"But you must not think so, or you wouldn't be questioning me."

"Nothing's definite at this point. We're just checking all the possibilities."

Which still didn't explain why they'd bothered to look her up, unless the FBI had a lot of manpower with nothing to do. And she didn't buy that.

"Were you ever in the basement?" Jack asked, in that same friendly tone that was beginning to get on her nerves.

"No." Which wasn't exactly true. She'd been there hundreds of times in her nightmares. But she wasn't going to bring all her childhood terrors out for their entertainment, not when she didn't know one thing that could help them and had the distinct feeling they were trying to manipulate her.

"Did you hear other kids talk about the basement?"

"I heard rumors of what it was like."

"What did you hear?"

"That it was cold and dark and teeming with big, gray rats." She crossed then uncrossed her legs, wishing they'd either get to the point or leave. "If you're going to talk to every person who ever lived at Meyers Bickham, you're going to be very busy."

"I imagine we will be."

The door from Kendra's bedroom squeaked open. "Mommy, can I come in here? I'm tired of watching the movie."

"Not yet, sweetie. I need to talk business with these men for a few more minutes. I won't be long."

"Okay, 'cause I'm hungry and I'm ready for my snack."

"I really don't know a thing that can help you," Sara said once Kendra had closed the door behind her. "And there's no sense in wasting any more of your time or mine."

"We just have a few more questions."

"No." She surprised herself with her audacity, with the FBI no less, but she really didn't like these men and she wasn't entirely sure why. "I'd like you to go now. You can leave me your cards and if I think of anything to help in your investigation, I'll call you."

"We came a long way to talk to you. We need your full cooperation in this. You understand what we mean, don't you?"

Sara tensed, then turned at footsteps on the porch.

Nat came to the door, the scythe he'd been carrying this morning in his right hand. Even now, he looked a bit like a man capable of a massacre. Obviously Jack thought so, too. He stood and shoved his hands into his pockets.

"Come on in, Nat," she said, thrilled at his timing. "My guests are just leaving, aren't you, gentlemen?"

Nat flashed her a questioning look, then seemed to pick up on what was going on. The man might be a lot of things, but he was definitely not stupid. He swung the screen door open and stepped inside, running a finger along the sharp edge of the scythe blade.

"We appreciate your time," Bruce said, heading for the door with an obviously forced smile on his face. Jack left right behind him.

"You okay?" Nat asked.

"Yeah. Yeah, I am." What a difference a day made. This morning Nat had given her a panic attack. This afternoon he seemed a lot safer and more trustworthy than the FBI. And she owed him big time for all he'd done, not the least of which was giving the FBI guys a little taste of their own intimidation methods.

"They were here to question me about a situation at the old Meyers Bickham Children's Home. I did live there for awhile, but I don't know anything that could help them. I told them that, but I got the feeling they didn't believe me."

He nodded, apparently not interested in knowing more. Which was fine with her. "Tell me, Nat. Do recluses ever accept dinner invitations?"

"I don't know. I don't remember getting one since I moved up to the mountains."

"Then this will be a first. Actually it will be a first for me, too. I've never invited a man with a beard for dinner, but I'd love to have you join Kendra and me tonight—if you'd like to, that is. It's the only way I know to repay you for your help."

He hesitated, and she was pretty sure he was going to say no.

"You don't owe me anything."

"Then come because we'd like to have you. I mean, you have to eat."

He brushed his hair back from his face with his free hand and nailed her with that stare that seemed more probing than a surgeon's knife. "I can come to dinner, but don't expect anything from me, Sara. I mean, don't read qualities into me that don't exist. I helped because you needed it. That's all."

"Dinner's it, Nat. And nothing fancy. I'm thinking meatloaf and potatoes and green beans."

"What time?"

"How's seven?"

"Seven it is."

And that was it. He took his scythe and left. And she wouldn't expect anything from Nat. The nice part was he wouldn't expect anything from her, either.

NAT STOOD under the shower, massaging the shampoo into his hair and letting the hot water pour down his naked body. He'd agreed to dinner in a weak moment. Helping out with manual labor was one thing, but making casual conversation over meatloaf would require a set of skills he wasn't sure he had any longer.

Not that he'd ever planned to become the social derelict he'd become. He'd tried to go on with life, but there hadn't been a life to go on with. A worthless leg. A raging guilt. A heart that had dried up like an apple left in the scorching Georgia sun.

So he'd slunk away like a wounded bear and wound up here in a rambling seventy-five-year-old house and an apple orchard.

He rinsed the shampoo from his hair and the slick layers of soap from beneath his arms and stepped onto the worn bath mat. Grabbing a towel, he rubbed briskly then looped it around his waist. Using the palm of his hand he wiped the vapor from the mirror and stared at his reflection.

He didn't really know the man who stared back at him. The long hair, the beard, the sun-bronzed skin and the wrinkles around the eyes. Thirty-eight years old, but he could have been a hundred.

And here he was, a stranger in a body that had changed so much he didn't even recognize it, going calling on a woman crazy enough to invite him.

A woman who'd been visited by two slick FBI agents this afternoon. She didn't look like the kind who'd eat a grape in the supermarket before it was paid for, so he had a hard time believing she'd done something worthy of their attention. But whatever she'd done or hadn't done, he had no intention of getting pulled into it.

Nat worked the comb through his hair. He was tempted to take the scissors and whack it off, but that might make Sara think he was sprucing up for her and he definitely didn't want to give her any ideas like that.

She was pretty, though, and he got the impression that she didn't know it. Long legs. Nice butt. Inviting lips. He felt a tightening in his groin, but luckily dread shot through him and killed the feeling before it got a chance to really get started.

It had been three and a half years since he'd been with a woman. He tried not to even think about it these days. And he damn sure didn't want to think about it tonight.

He combed his hair and dressed in clean jeans and a blue sport shirt. It was only six-thirty, too early to show up at Sara's. He flicked on his TV and tuned in the evening news. News and an occasional ball game was about all he watched, though he had a dish and could pick up any channel he wanted.

He started to the kitchen for a glass of water but stopped when he heard the words Meyers Bickham. He listened to the sketchy details about the bones that had been discovered while construction workers were tearing down the old orphanage east of Dahlonega. *Two days ago.*

Two days ago, and Sara had visitors from the FBI today. It seemed a little unlikely. Actually it seemed a lot unlikely. The wheels of bureaucracy did not turn that fast, especially when they were dealing with an old crime that didn't involve immediate danger.

Didn't matter. Wasn't his battle. He'd lost his a long time ago. Tonight it was just meatloaf and awkwardness and an experiment in futility that couldn't end too soon.

THE MAN HELD the cell phone to his ear, trying hard to hear above the static. "We talked to Sara Murdoch."

More static. He drove to the top of the incline and pulled onto the shoulder. "What did you say? I couldn't hear you."

"I asked what you found out."

"She claims not to know anything, or at least not to remember anything, but I don't know. She plays the innocent routine well, but she's a sly one. Might have been lying. I couldn't tell."

"Can't see any reason she'd lie to the FBI."

"I just know how it seemed. Other thing is, it's not just her and her daughter up at that cabin."

"Who else was there?"

"Some wild-looking mountain man. He had a scythe and from the looks of him I'd say he'd just as soon slice off a head or two as not."

"A mountain man. There's no accounting for the tastes of some of those college professors."

"So what do you want us to do?"

"I'll have to think about it. I may have to make a call on Mrs. Murdoch myself."

"She won't be glad to see you. She made no secret of the fact that Meyers Bickham is not near and dear to her heart."

"Nor to mine. But neither is Sara Murdoch."

"Gotcha."

THE PORCH SWING creaked in harmony with the tree frogs, cicadas and the occasional hoot of an owl and the croak of a bullfrog. Sara sipped her coffee, amazed that dinner had gone so well. There had been little of the awkward silences she'd feared, mainly because Kendra had taken advantage of having two members in her captive audience.

But Kendra was in bed now, and Nat was sitting on the top step of the porch, leaning against the post and staring into the darkness. She was surprised he'd stayed for coffee, had been even more surprised that he'd cleaned up the kitchen while she'd gotten Kendra down for the night.

"It's incredibly peaceful out here," Sara said.

"Quiet, anyway."

"I'm not sure I'd like it all the time, though. I'd miss the restaurants and stores. Mostly I'd miss having friends."

"It takes some getting used to."

"But you must like it. You've stayed for three years."

He shrugged but didn't answer. She was pushing, making him uncomfortable. She dropped the attempt at conversation and tried to just enjoy the moment. Instead her mind wandered to the situation at Meyers Bickham.

"You seemed upset when the two men from the FBI left."

The remark surprised Sara. In fact she'd almost expected Nat to get up and leave without saying another word. "I didn't like their attitude."

"Were they here to ask you about the bodies uncovered at the orphanage?"

"Yeah." She shuddered. Hard not to when she thought about the basement of the orphanage being a mausoleum for dead infants. Unless... "You don't suppose it was some kind of abortion clinic at one time and that what they found was the remains of fetuses?"

"No. From what I saw on the news tonight, the remains are from at least full-term newborns, maybe even older."

"Then there must be a record somewhere of who's buried there. Old church records. Court records. Something."

"You'd think. What did you tell the two guys who were here this afternoon?"

"That I didn't know anything about the bodies. They didn't seem convinced. They asked if I'd been in the basement before."

"And had you?"

"No…at least, not when I was awake."

His brows arched. "Were you a sleepwalker?"

She shouldn't have said anything, but now that she had, she felt a strange need to talk about the nightmares. "I didn't sleepwalk, but I had trouble adjusting to the orphanage. I started having horrible nightmares. I'd wake up at night screaming that there was a ghost baby in the basement and that it was crying for me."

"Had you been in the basement?"

"I thought I had." She closed her eyes and tried to work through the haze that clouded her memories. "I thought I'd seen a parade in the basement—a parade of ghosts. Fortunately there was one person at the orphanage, a doctor, who seemed to understand what I was going through. She talked to me for hours and gave me some kind of pills to help me. I didn't know what they were then, but I suppose they were something to control my anxiety."

"And she convinced you that the ghosts were nightmares?"

"Oh, they were nightmares. Over and over. I still have them sometimes, but mostly I just hear the ghost baby cry. Especially when I'm stressed. It's ironic that in my nightmares I was convinced the basement was haunted. Now it turns out it held dead bodies."

Nat grew quiet again. That didn't surprise her, but his questions and interest in her past had.

He stood, stepped closer, then leaned his backside against the porch railing. "I don't think those men were from the FBI, Sara."

"They showed me their IDs."

"IDs are easy to come by. A good forger can make one even an expert can't tell from the real thing."

And she was no expert. She hadn't looked at them closely, wasn't certain Bruce had even shown her his. "Why do you think they were imposters?"

"Timing. The FBI doesn't react that quickly in a nonemergency situation. I doubt they've even been called in yet. There's no evidence at this point of an interstate crime or anything that can't be handled by local authorities."

"But if they weren't from the FBI, who were they?"

"Maybe an interested party trying to find out if you know something that can incriminate them."

"Geez! You've given this some thought, haven't you?"

"Just stating the obvious."

It hadn't been obvious to her. Maybe that's what Nat did during all those hours he spent alone. Dreamed up paranoid theories and hid from little green men with radar guns pointed at him.

Only, Nat seemed much more believable than the two men who'd sat in the cabin this afternoon and asked her questions that made no sense. And then there was the note she'd received before she left Columbus. She wondered what Nat would make of that.

Since he was already this deep into her problems, she might as well get his opinion on that as well.

"I have something I'd like you to read."

He nodded.

She went to her bedroom and pulled the note from her handbag. She picked up the flashlight by the bed on her way out. It wouldn't draw bugs the way the porch light would. She handed them both to Nat, then stood next to him as he read it.

"Someone is convinced that you know something about the bodies."

"But that's crazy. I lived in the orphanage five years and I don't remember one baby dying."

"But there were babies there?"

"Of course, but most weren't there very long. They were adopted quickly. People love babies. It was skinny, freckle-faced ten-year-olds that no one wanted."

The anger and pain crept into her voice. The old hurts. From so long ago, but still hanging around to ambush her when she least expected it.

"I don't know anything. I can't imagine where the dead babies came from or when they were buried, or how many graves they're talking about."

"Eight so far."

"I'm still not sure what the crime is," Sara said. "As creepy as it all is, it could just be that the basement was only used as a crypt."

"Or it could be that the babies were murdered."

Sara held on to the railing for support, suddenly feeling weak and nauseous. "They didn't kill babies at Meyers Bickham, Nat. It was an orphanage."

"You don't seem to have a lot of good memories of the place other than the doctor who gave you drugs and convinced you that your nightmares were remnants of hallucinations.''

''I don't have any good memories of Meyers Bickham. The caretakers were strict and punishing and made me feel as if I were a piece of trash that no one wanted. But they never physically hurt me. It was only my spirit they wounded.''

She turned away. She was getting too emotional, revealing things about herself that Nat didn't need to know. They weren't even friends. They were barely acquaintances.

''I could be wrong, Sara. Maybe the guys were from the FBI and they're just looking for any information they can pick up from people who lived at the orphanage.''

But he didn't believe that. If he had he'd never have approached the subject. He was restless now, shuffling his feet, looking away.

''I guess it's time to call it a night,'' she said. ''Thanks again for all you've done.'' She touched his arm. He pulled away as if her hand had been hot. She'd overstepped the fragile boundaries he needed.

He turned and walked away without looking at her, then stopped on the bottom step.

''Be careful, Sara. I don't have a phone, but if you need anything, come to my place. Just turn in at the first drive off Delringer Road.''

She watched him until he disappeared from sight, amazed at his invitation, but frightened by it as well. If he'd made an offer like that he must believe she could be in danger. Just what she needed to have hanging over her out here in her isolated cabin.

But he had to be wrong. She didn't know a thing and she would not let those faceless demons from her past sneak back into her life. She was not a help-less kid any longer. Still, she might just go to the hardware store in Dahlonega tomorrow and pick up some latches for the window.

SARA WOKE to the shrill ring of her cell phone. She rubbed the sleep from her eyes and turned to face the clock. One-thirty. Good news never came by phone at one-thirty in the morning. She didn't have to answer it.

Only she would. There was something about a ringing phone in the middle of the night that wouldn't let you ignore it. She picked it up and murmured a sleepy hello.

"Sara Murdoch?"

"Yes?"

"Sara Thomas Murdoch?"

"Yes."

"Hello, Sara. Welcome back to the nightmare."

Chapter Five

It was a man's voice but not one she recognized. Her heart raced, her body and mind caught in the clutches of dread. This couldn't be happening, not again. She was thirty years old. She was a mother. The crazy fears that had haunted her when she was ten couldn't just swoop into her life like some vicious bird of prey. "Who is this?"

"Keep silent, Sara."

"Keep silent about what? I don't know what you're talking about."

"You'll figure it out."

Damn. The decayed bodies might as well be falling into her hands. "I don't know anything to tell."

"Good. Because if you talk, your body will be the next one found."

And then the connection was broken.

She didn't know how long she lay there, staring at the ceiling and feeling numb. Finally she forced her legs over the side of the bed and went to check on her daughter.

Kendra was fast asleep, and still not totally quiet. She murmured something Sara couldn't make out, then rolled over and rummaged for the stuffed bear that had become lost in the covers. All that without even opening her eyes.

So precious. So trusting.

Sara walked over and kissed her lightly on the cheek. *I won't let you down, sweetheart. I won't drag you into my nightmares. I won't let this touch your life.*

But the words twisted inside her as she stepped away from the bed. That was the same promise her mother had made to her just before she walked out of her life and left Sara totally alone.

Sara walked back to the bedroom, collapsed onto the side of the bed, and picked up her cell phone. She hated to beg, but surely Steven would see the necessity of this. After all, Kendra was his daughter, too.

''Hello.''

''Hi, Steven. It's Sara.''

''I know who you are, Sara. What's wrong? Is it Kendra?''

''Yes. You have to take her for the summer, Steven. I know you have plans, but you'll just have to change them.''

''It's the middle of the night. Are you drunk or just gone totally looney?''

''Neither. My life has gotten really complicated, maybe even dangerous, and I need you to take Kendra for a while.''

''What the hell are you talking about?''

She told him about the note, the visit from the men from the FBI and the phone call.

''Meyers Bickham. I should have known.''

''I don't know who's threatening me or what he

or the FBI think I know, but I can't take any chances with Kendra's safety.''

"This isn't about Kendra. It's about you and your hang ups with your past.''

"This isn't something I dreamed up, Steven. The bones and skulls are real.''

"But the paranoia is yours, Sara. You drag your past around like some ball and chain and let it ruin everything you do.''

"I know what you think of me, Steven, but I'm not asking this for myself. All I want you to do is accept your responsibility as a father. Take Kendra and keep her safe, if not for the summer, then at least for a couple of weeks.''

"If I thought for a second Kendra was in danger, I'd get out of bed and start down there this minute, but she's not. The FBI agents told you they were just doing routine questioning.''

"And the note and the phone call?''

"Didn't even mention Meyers Bickham. They were probably from one of your students, trying to scare you, pay you back for failing them or giving them a hard time this past semester. It happens all the time. Remember that time my car got egged because I made that jackass fullback sit out a game?''

"Kendra's not a car, Steven.''

"You know what I mean. And if you think about it, you know damn well no one's going to go out and do bodily harm to everyone who lived at that orphanage just to keep them quiet.''

"So the answer is no?''

"I'm leaving the country next week. The plans are all made.''

"And what about your daughter?''

"Stay in the mountain cabin with her, Sara. Get some rest and have some fun. And forget that damned orphanage."

"Have some fun. That should solve everything."

"Give Kendra a hug for me. Tell her Daddy loves her."

"Sure. I'll tell her."

Sara broke the connection and dropped the phone onto the bed. She felt washed out, depleted of even the dread and anger that had driven her minutes before. She didn't buy everything Steven had said, but she couldn't deny that some of it made sense.

Hundreds of children had lived in Meyers Bickham over the years. Even if someone was running scared, he couldn't go around killing everyone who'd ever lived there.

Sara got out of bed again and padded to the kitchen in her bare feet. She filled a glass with bottled water and drank it slowly while her mind scanned the events of the past two days, like a video being fast-forwarded. But it slowed at the point where Nat had sat on her front porch after dinner, drinking coffee and staring at the stars.

Supposedly he was a recluse, but in two short days they'd connected in some indefinable way. She knew so little about him, but she knew he didn't fit the simple mountain man image he portrayed. He was complicated, like a painting that constantly reflected new depth and definition, defying interpretation.

Still, she couldn't believe she'd told him about the nightmares and the threats. Or that she was standing here right now, thinking about him and wondering if she'd see him again.

NAT WADED through the high grass beneath his Ozark Gold trees, doing some thinning but mostly searching for signs of insect damage. Routine work that unfortunately didn't calm his mind.

He'd fallen asleep last night thinking of the woman who'd barely left his mind for the past three and a half years. Maria. Even saying her name had been intoxicating back then. But then so had everything about her.

Long black hair that sifted like silk through his fingers. Narrow hips that swayed seductively when she walked. The mesmerizing feel of her deft fingers stroking his body. Her hands on his skin, forbidden and subtly exotic.

But then he'd wakened in the middle of the night, and it had been Sara's face that had popped into his mind.

There was nothing subtle about Sara. Her emotions jumped out at him. Fear, aggravation, pleasure, whatever she felt. Her eyes and body language telegraphed every variance.

He pulled a couple of apples from a low branch above him, leaving room for the ones he left to grow fuller and rounder. He dropped the fruit into his canvas hip basket and gingerly brushed away a honeybee that hovered around his hand. Bees were his best pollinators and he didn't want to harm this one.

He walked farther, high boots sinking in the soft earth, trying to concentrate on apples and failing miserably. He should have never gone against his better judgment and agreed to show Sara and Kendra to the cabin two nights ago. And he definitely shouldn't have gone back yesterday.

Then he wouldn't have known about those two

guys who'd come calling. Wouldn't have connected Sara with the investigation at that old orphanage. But he had and now he may as well admit that there was no way he could just walk away.

Giving up on the pretense that this was a normal day, he stomped back to the house and straddled his bike. There was a pay phone at Mattie's. A direct connection with the life he'd left behind.

"NAT SANDERSON. Now this is a surprise."

Bob Eggars sounded the same as always, but then he was. It was Nat who had changed. "How's business?"

"Busier than ever. Are you ready to come back to work?"

"No." And even if he were he doubted there was a demand for limping agents. "I'm just looking for a little information."

"I suppose we're not talking about apples."

"No."

"Sounds like you're coming back to life down there in that sleepy Georgia orchard. And if you want my opinion, it's about damn time. What do you want to know?"

"Whether or not the Bureau's involved in the Meyers Bickham situation."

"That's right. The dead babies in the walls are down in your neck of the woods, aren't they?"

"Fairly close."

"So are you in the game or just curious?"

"Curious."

"That's a start. I can find out and get back to you. Did you ever get a phone?"

"No, but I can call you back."

"Okay. Give me an hour."

"You got it."

BOB EGGERS glanced at his daily calendar as he made the call to his buddy in the Georgia office. This was a no-sweat favor. The Bureau was either in on the investigation or they weren't and it would be a matter of public record.

But a call from Nat Sanderson was a big deal. The guy had been one of the best agents who'd ever worked for Bob. He'd had that natural ability to take one look and assess everything about a situation. It was as if the guy could smell danger.

Those same skills had worked for him in the private security business after he'd left the Bureau. Until a woman had screwed up his life so completely that he'd crawled into a cave to lick his wounds and forgot to come out again. Which made Bob wonder what had caused this sudden and unexpected turnaround. If a woman was behind it, he only hoped she was nothing like Maria Hernandez.

SARA SPENT the morning with Kendra. They drove to Amicolola Falls State Park and took one of the easy hikes. It was a perfect day for it. Cooler than yesterday, with leftover raindrops from a predawn shower dripping from the trees and splattering on their noses, making Kendra giggle. They'd had an early lunch at the lodge dining room, then stopped by Mattie's on the way home for an ice-cream cone.

The perfect late May day had it not been for the undercurrent of apprehension and indecision that accompanied Sara's every move. She didn't buy Steven's idea that the threats had been from a student, and if the call last night had been a serious threat, then an isolated cabin in the woods might not be the best place to be. Except that only a few people knew she was here. On the other hand, the FBI had found her.

If they were the FBI.

If she only had a clue who'd made the call. But it was ludicrous for anyone to think she knew anything that could hurt them. She'd been part of the powerless majority, ordered around and punished for the slightest infraction.

So whoever had issued the threat really was clueless.

Sara took the last of the chenille spreads from the washer and carried it out to the makeshift clothesline she's strung between two trees. The cabin was really shaping up. It would be a shame to have to move out after all the work she'd put into the place over the past two days.

They even had a new footbridge. And a fierce-looking neighbor with a scythe she could sic on FBI agents who'd overstayed their welcome. If Nat had lifted his hand at that point and swung the scythe, dimpled Bruce would have probably jumped through the open window and be running yet.

For the first time that day she laughed. Actually, now that she thought about it, it might have been the first time in weeks that she'd laughed out loud at anything other than Kendra's antics.

Totally weird that it would be connected to a bearded recluse who'd scared her half to death a little over twenty-four hours ago and a couple of FBI agents with attitudes.

She fastened the last clothespin, then had the unsettling feeling that someone was watching her. Talk about mood swings. She spun around. Nat was crossing the drawbridge, his limp more evident than it had been since she'd met him. There was no scythe this time, but he was carrying a gallon jug of something and he was indeed staring at her.

"You seem to be in a good mood," he said, walking toward her.

"I'm working on it." She wiped her damp hands on the rough denim of her shorts. "I'm surprised to see you back so soon."

"I brought you some apple cider. It's from last year's crop of apples."

"Thanks. I'm sure we'll enjoy it." He didn't hand it to her, just stood there, mouth drawn so tight that his lips all but disappeared beneath the beard. "The cider's not the only reason I came by."

His voice had taken on an edge and he stared at the cider as if it were some flammable mixture that might blow up in his hand at any moment.

"So, hit me with the worst."

"I talked to a friend of mine today about the men who came to question you yesterday."

Geez! He'd probably mentioned this to Mattie. The woman was nice, but she was a talker. Everyone from Dahlonega to the Appalachian Trail probably knew by now that Sara had been questioned by the FBI.

"I'd prefer you not discuss my business with the FBI with anyone, Nat."

"Your business wasn't with the FBI."

"I know you think that, Nat, but…"

"The FBI is not involved in the Meyers Bickham investigation at the present time. That's not my opinion, Sara. It's a fact. I checked. If you don't believe me, pick up your cell phone and call the Georgia FBI office. Ask them if they sent anyone out to question you.''

Sara started to argue, but the useless words stuck in her throat. She reached for the chenille spread that swayed in the wind and knotted the fabric in her hands, holding on to it while she fought the frustration and pricks of fear that wouldn't quit.

Nat put his hands on her shoulders. His touch was awkward and tentative. Probably a good thing, because with the least bit of encouragement, she'd have thrown herself into his arms and held on tight. That surely would have sent him running.

''Do you want to go inside and talk about it?'' Nat asked, dropping his hands from her shoulders.

''I'd like to talk, but not inside. I don't want Kendra to hear and she's set up a playhouse for her dolls in the living room.''

''Then let's sit on the porch. I'll get you a glass of cider.''

''Why are you doing this, Nat?''

''Because it's too hot out here in the sun and I'm thirsty.''

''Why are you getting involved in my problems?'' It's…it's unrecluse-like.''

''I'm a fool for meatloaf.''

NAT LISTENED to the account of last night's bizarre phone call and the following call to Kendra's father. What a jerk. But then, the guy had to be a little crazy to have walked away from Sara and Kendra.

''It's so frustrating,'' Sara said. ''I don't know anything, and yet someone seems convinced that I do. And even that wouldn't be so bad if I wasn't afraid that Kendra is going to get drawn into this.''

''Do you think much about the time you spent in the orphanage?''

''I've spent most of my adult life trying not to think about it.'' She turned away from him, but she was tangling her hands in her lap, and he could see the strain on her face. ''You think it's possible I know something, too, don't you?''

''I'm not sure it matters at this point. The fact that someone believes that you do not only involves you in the investigation, but puts you in danger.''

She took a deep breath and exhaled slowly. ''I'd hoped this would just blow over, but if those men yesterday weren't from the FBI then I need to report all of this to the police. And then I'll go back to Columbus. Kendra will be safer there.''

''Not necessarily.''

''Well, I can't stay here in an isolated cabin.''

''There's another option.'' And he was out of his mind to even think of it. Crazier yet if he offered it.

The front door squeaked open and Kendra peeked through it. ''Hi, Mr. Nat.''

''Hello, Kendra.''

''Do you want me to help you hammer something?''

''Not today. Everything's fixed.''

''Mr. Nat and I are talking about something very important, Kendra. Play with your dolls for another minute, and then I'll come in and get you a snack.''

''Oreos?''

''If that's what you want.''

''I do, and some milk. Do you want some Oreos, Mr. Nat?''

"Oreos sound great."

Nat could hear Kendra singing in her high-pitched voice as she went back to her dolls. Totally innocent, the same as Maria's daughter had been. In the end, it hadn't made a bit of difference. He swallowed hard, knowing he didn't have a chance against this kind of pressure. So he opened his mouth and forced the words through three and a half years of regret.

"Move in with me, Sara. Move in with me, and I'll keep both of you safe."

Chapter Six

Sara's mouth fell open. Those were the last words she'd have expected to come from Nat's mouth. The absurdity of it was beyond belief. "I can't stay with you."

"It was just an idea."

"We barely know each other," she said, feeling she had to explain her response even though he'd shrugged it off as inconsequential.

"People move in with people they don't know all the time," he said, "but it's your decision."

He was right, of course. Renters, sometimes roommates, but she couldn't do it, not with a man like Nat.

A man like Nat. Helpful. Considerate. A bearded recluse. It would be awkward and...and the strange awareness that existed between them might intensify.

But if she packed up and went home she'd be giving up her vacation. Kendra would be upset. And Raye Ann had probably already moved into her apartment, thinking she'd have it to herself.

She had to be nuts for even thinking of taking him up on this offer. But then again, why not? She'd be safer with him, especially if he kept that scythe handy. Who'd dare go up against him?

Still, she was sure Nat didn't know what he was getting into. "We'd be in your space. It would be a totally different life than you're used to."

"It's a big house."

"People will talk."

He tugged on his beard. "Probably."

Not that he cared what people thought of him. And she was only here for the summer. "Are you sure you want us, Nat?"

"You'll be safe."

That wasn't the answer she'd been looking for, but it was what this was all about. "We can try it," she said.

"Then get a few things together. I'll be back to help you move them this afternoon." He started to leave, then stopped. "Don't call the sheriff yet."

"Why not?"

"I want to check out a few things first."

He didn't wait for an answer, just turned and strode away. She'd agreed to move in with him one minute and he was giving orders the next. She watched him walk away, hoping she hadn't just made a very big mistake in agreeing to sleep in the rambling house of a mountain man who seemed to have as many facets to his personality as he had apples in his orchard.

But right now he was the safest game in town.

Judge Cary Arnold sat at a table in the back corner of the bar in his Atlanta country club and lifted the glass of scotch to his lips. He didn't usually drink hard liquor before the cocktail hour, but he needed it today. He finished his drink and had ordered a second by the time Abigail strode across the room and took the chair opposite him.

"Sorry I'm late. There was an emergency at the hospital."

"You could have called," Cary said.

"I could have canceled. This meeting is a waste of time anyway."

"That's your opinion."

"You're getting bent out of shape over nothing, Cary. Sara's not going to say anything. She doesn't know anything."

"She was there, Abigail. She knows."

"I told you at the time that she didn't understand what she saw. She was only ten years old." Abigail stopped talking and smiled as the waiter approached them.

"What can I get you, Dr. Harrington?"

"A vodka martini. Very dry. With two olives."

Cary tilted his drink, swirling the ice and liquid, not saying anything until the waiter was out of earshot. "I heard today that the FBI may be called in on this. If they are, that will change things considerably."

"I don't see why."

"They'll question me."

"Then I suggest you get your story straight."

"I don't have a story."

"Sure you do." Abigail reached across the table and put her hand on his. "You're shocked at the discovery. Your dealings with the staff there had always been positive, and the children in residence were well cared for."

"You make this sound so simple. But then you always did."

"Because I don't leave things to chance. The groundwork was laid long ago."

"I hope so, Abigail. I sincerely hope so. Because if I go down, you are going with me. I promise you that."

A foursome came in from the golf course and took a table not far from theirs. Abigail changed gears abruptly, jumping into an animated monologue about a new art gallery that had just opened in town.

Once the waiter had returned with her drink, she took a few sips, then rose to leave, explaining she needed to get back to the hospital and assuring him again that everything was under control.

And it was for her. Beautiful, confident, rich Abigail. She knew all about laying the groundwork. She'd done it in her own life and had managed to get everything she wanted.

At one time, Cary had thought that included him. Proof of what a naive fool he'd been.

But he wasn't going to be a fool this time. And he wasn't leaving it all up to Abigail.

BY THE TIME Nat returned to help load the van, Sara was feeling really down about leaving the cabin in the woods. With the dead bugs, layers of dust and spiderwebs cleared out, it was cozy and charming. The perfect vacation habitat for someone who wasn't getting threatening phone calls in the middle of the night and surprise visits from fake FBI agents.

Nat had talked very little since he'd returned to help her move into his house. She hoped he wasn't having second thoughts, because she couldn't deal with any more decisions today.

"C'mon, Mommy. You're too slow."

"I'm coming."

"I think we should take our new bridge with us," Kendra said as she trotted along after Nat.

"No room," he answered as he lifted the last load into the back of Sara's van. "Besides, we won't need it."

"Don't you have a stream at your house?"

"I do, but I already have a bridge, one big enough to drive a truck over. I have a pond, too."

"Does it have fish in it?"

"A few. I have a dog, too. A chocolate lab named Mackie."

Kendra's eyes lit up. "Can I play with him?"

"I expect you'll have to. He'll make sure of it."

"I hope he likes me."

"Give him a few pats, toss a ball for him to chase and take him swimming and he'll love you."

"Do you have a swimming pool?"

"Nope. A swimming hole."

"You swim in a hole? In the ground?"

"Sure do."

"Mommy, can we go swimming in Mr. Nat's hole?"

"We'll see."

"When will we see?"

"We have to unpack first."

"But after that, can we?"

"We'll swim. I'm not sure when."

Sara stopped at the bridge and looked back at the cabin. She'd had such high hopes for the summer when she'd left Columbus. No cares. No worries. She should have known it was too good to last.

"Are you ready?" Nat asked.

"Are you?"

"Guess there's only one way to find out."

There was no missing the note of panic in his voice.

SARA STOOD on the back porch looking out over the orchard that grew on the hilly terrain behind the house. Nat had persuaded her to call the sheriff in charge of the Meyers Bickham investigation instead of the local one. Meyers Bickham was in the north-west corner of the state, not far from the borders of Alabama and Tennessee. Sheriff Troy Wesley had seemed eager to talk to her, and it turned out he was in the Dahlonega area visiting a friend and was now bookin' it over to Nat's.

"The sheriff's here," Nat announced, sticking his head out the door. "He's waiting in the living room. Are you ready to see him?"

"As ready as I'll ever be. Just let me check on Kendra first and make certain she's still involved in the movie."

"Take your time. I'll keep him company, but he's not going anywhere. He's hoping you're the lead he's been looking for."

"You almost sound like a cop yourself."

"Not me. I just grow apples."

He might grow fruit, but she was certain that didn't begin to describe the man whose house she'd just moved into. Rugged and mysterious. Talked when he wanted, ignored questions when he didn't.

And had eyes that could reach inside her and turn her inside out.

She had the urge to grab Kendra, jump in the van and drive until even she didn't know where she was. Away from Nat. Away from threats. Away from cops.

Only there was no running away from her past. She knew. She'd tried.

TWO HOURS LATER, Sheriff Troy Wesley crawled back in his squad car and drove away. Nat was undecided if the man had any leads as to who had buried the babies in the brick wall, but he'd definitely asked Sara a lot of questions about the time she'd lived there.

"Now that's what I call the third degree," Sara said, massaging the tendons in her neck and stretching her long legs in front of her. "The guy knows me better now than I know myself."

"He didn't take a lot of notes, though, so I'm not sure if he was looking for information or trying to catch you in a lie."

"That's an interesting take."

"To be expected, though. He figures if someone went to the trouble of pretending to be FBI agents just so they could question you, there's a good chance you know something."

"I'd say you're right. He was fascinated with my account of those two men."

"Obviously they weren't anyone he's questioned yet in the investigation. Of course, the investigation is just getting started. Something like this can go on for months—or years."

"Thanks for sharing that, partner."

Partner. She was teasing, of course, but it troubled him all the same, brought back the realization that he was stepping up to the plate again with the memory of the last strikeout still firmly in his mind.

"I don't think the sheriff gave much credence to the note or the phone call."

"I found it hard to tell what he thinks," Nat admitted, "except that you're nuts for staying in the house with me."

"He didn't say that."

"He might as well have."

"He doesn't know you. Not that I do. You hardly talk about anything, and you never talk about yourself. Why is that? Why do you insist on being such a mystery man?"

"Let it go, Sara."

"I don't like the rules in our relationship, Nat. We can talk about me, but not about you. I'm an open book. You're top secret."

"We don't have a relationship, Sara. Someone threatened you and Kendra. I offered to protect you."

"So basically you're my bodyguard. Is that it, Nat?"

"Basically."

"Then I guess we should talk money. How much do bodyguards make? Ten dollars an hour? Or do you get paid by the job?"

Tension filled the room, thick and choking. She was falling apart and he knew he was only a small part of her frustration. He had to get out of here before he did something he'd be sorry for. Like take her in his arms and hold her.

He stood and walked to the front door.

"I just want to know one thing, Nat. I know you

offered your house on the spur of the minute. Do you still want me here?''

He held on to the door, feeling as if the past were crashing in on him. The flying bullets. The screams. The body.

''I want you here, Sara.'' And then he was out the door before she saw the real him, the shattered shell of the man he'd been.

NAT STOOD in front of the bathroom mirror, wrapped in a towel and staring at his hair. It was still damp from the shower, but it hung over his ears and crawled around his neck like some disgusting, hairy bug. He should go in Dahlonega and find a barber. Such a simple thing, but he hadn't had a commercial haircut since he'd bought the orchard. He'd whacked at it a few times himself, but that was it.

Hell, until Sara had moved in four days ago, he'd hardly even noticed it. He'd pretty much avoided the mirror. Amazing how well you could do that when the only place you had to go was the grocers or to the hardware store for supplies.

Now mirrors seemed to ambush him every time he got near one. Not that Sara said anything about his disheveled appearance. In fact she'd made no mention of anything personal since their run-in after the sheriff left.

He was the protector. She was the protectee. It was the way it had to be. And even that was asking way more than he'd ever thought he'd have to give again.

But he had to have more from her. He knew she hated to talk about Meyers Bickham, but he needed feedback. He'd called on his sources for a list of people who'd worked at the orphanage or had been involved in its administration during the years that Sara was a resident there. They were even supplying some pictures, all to be delivered by overnight mail.

Not that he was playing cop, as Bob had accused him of doing. It was just that he liked knowing what he was up against.

He stared into the mirror again, then opened the cabinet behind it and pulled out a pair of scissors. Lifting a wad of hair off his neck, he whacked off about four inches. That got it up to just beneath his earlobe.

He whacked a few more times, doing the back by feel. It was a little uneven, but it looked... Who was he kidding? It looked pathetic. And he looked repulsive. Not that it mattered. It was probably all the better if Sara thought of him as a bestial recluse. Heaven help him if she were ever to show any sexual interest in him.

He pulled on the pajama bottoms, another of the concessions he'd made to having a woman and a kid in the house. No more running around in the nude, though he still slept that way.

He walked through the quiet house to the kitchen, then stopped when he noticed Sara standing at the window. Her red hair was down from the ponytail, full and loose and falling about the shoulders of a pale pink nightshirt that reached just above her knees.

His heart clattered around in his chest, and his mouth got so dry he had to try several times before he could swallow. She turned around and started talking. He heard the words but couldn't concentrate—and couldn't stop staring.

Her face was fresh-scrubbed, all pink and shiny.

And he could see the outline of her nipples pressed against the soft cotton fabric of her shirt.

Hair. She was talking about his hair.

"I can cut it for you if you like. I worked as a beautician for a while before I started at the university."

He swallowed hard, knowing he had to get past the desire that had waylaid him, and fast. "So you think my hair needs help, do you?"

She nodded. "Serious help."

"I'm game if you are."

"Great." She pulled one of the straight-backed kitchen chairs out and centered it under the light. "You have a seat, and I'll get my shears."

"Sure you don't want the scythe? It's a lot of hair."

"Not for the hair on your head, but if you let me at that beard...."

"One thing at a time."

He sat in the chair and waited, thinking he should back out of this before she stepped close and tangled her hands in his hair. But she was already back, scissors in hand. Looking like something from a wet dream. And he doubted he could have made his legs move if he'd had sense enough to run.

Chapter Seven

Sara spread a towel around Nat's shoulders, then lifted his hair with her fingers, letting the thick locks slide between her fingers. The hair was smooth and untangled, still damp from the shower. She could smell the shampoo and the soap—the same soap she'd showered with a half hour ago.

The kitchen grew warm, and all of a sudden the simple task of cutting Nat's hair seemed like an intimate experience.

It was the setting that was affecting her. A cozy kitchen. The hum of the air conditioner. Both of them in pajamas. It couldn't be more. But her hands trembled when they brushed the back of his sun-bronzed neck.

"If it's more than you bargained for, you can back out."

"No." Her voice was far more breathy than she'd intended. "How short do you want it?"

"I'm at your mercy."

"You are a brave man." Sara cut slowly, hoping her level of arousal would diminish as she worked. It didn't. Her hand lingered too long when it brushed his skin. Her heart beat too fast. And crazy trembles kept skittering across her nerve endings and swimming around in her stomach.

The whole experience seemed more like a sensual dance than a haircut. When she finished, she walked in front of him, stooped to eye level and checked to see if she'd gotten the sides somewhere near even. He looked different. Younger and surprisingly more virile than he had before.

"Not bad," she whispered.

"No. Not bad."

Only he couldn't see his hair. He was staring at her and she was drowning in the dark, inky pools of his eyes. He was going to kiss her, and she didn't want to think about all the reasons he shouldn't. She didn't want to think at all.

He cradled her face in his hands and pulled her closer.

"Mommy, can I have a drink of water?"

Sara jumped back so quickly she almost tripped over Nat's feet. Kendra was standing in the kitchen doorway, dragging her stuffed bear with one hand and rubbing her eyes with the other.

"Sure. I'll get it for you," she said, her breath coming in short, fast gasps.

"What happened to your hair, Mr. Nat?"

"Your mother cut it for me. I guess I better go see how it looks."

Sara heard his quickly departing footsteps as she got Kendra's water, but she didn't turn around. She handed Kendra the water, then held on to the edge of the counter while she tried to get her wits about her.

They'd almost made a big mistake—would have kissed, maybe more, if Kendra hadn't come in when she had. They'd gotten caught up in the moment, let normal sexual urges swell until they'd been consumed by them.

But it didn't mean a thing except that they were human. Living in the same house, sharing the one bathroom, talking over breakfast. It was bound to produce some sexual tension. They'd just have to be more careful to keep it under control.

They didn't have a relationship. Nat had made that clear. And she had more than enough problems with threats and the tumbling walls of Meyers Bickham.

Kendra took two sips of the water, then handed it back to Sara. "Will you come and read me another story?"

"It's very late, sweetheart, too late for stories, but I'll come and lie down with you for a few minutes."

"Okay."

Sara tucked Kendra in the big four-poster bed, then crawled in beside her. The moon shone through the window, painting silvery streaks across the sheets and her pink nightshirt.

Nat was only two doors down. He'd probably be crawling into bed now, too. She imagined his body sprawled across the bed... And she shouldn't be thinking of what she was thinking right now. She shouldn't, but she was. And wondering what would have happened if Kendra hadn't come walking into the kitchen when she had.

Would they have stopped with a kiss? Or would they have made love? And if they had, would she have ever been the same again?

"IT'S IMPORTANT," Nat said. "I wouldn't ask you to do this if it wasn't."

Sara dipped her hands back into the soapy dish-water, searching for another cereal bowl or orange juice glass to wash. Anything to put off the inevitable. "I promised Kendra I'd take her swimming this morning."

"You still can. I just need you to look over some names and pictures of people who worked at Meyers Bickham while you were there. An hour tops. That's all it will take."

But it wasn't the hour's delay that was bothering her. It was that even after fifteen years of being away from the orphanage, thinking about it still made her almost physically ill.

"You're not a cop, Nat, not part of the investigation. So what's the point in your digging into all of this?"

"It's standard bodyguard procedure."

"How would you know? You are an apple grower who got drafted into service—not that I don't appreciate your hospitality. I do, I just don't see the point in this."

"I can do a lot better job of protecting you if I know who I'm protecting you from."

"There hasn't been a threat of any kind since we moved in with you, and that's been five days now. Besides, the person who was bothering me is probably finally convinced I don't know anything."

"Could be."

"But you don't think so?"

He dried the last dish as she wiped out the sink. "I just think it's good to be prepared. I'll pour us another cup of coffee," Nat said, already pulling two clean mugs from the shelf.

"None for me. My stomach can't take it." It was

clear the guy wasn't going to take no for an answer. She went to the back door to check on Kendra. She was under the walnut tree that grew near the shed where Nat kept his supplies.

Evidently Mackie was supposed to be a horse for her dolls. The dog wasn't cooperating, but he turned around every now and then to lick Kendra's hand.

"She'll miss Mackie when we leave," Sara said.

"You should get her a puppy."

"We can't have pets in the apartment."

"So move to a house with a yard."

"I may have to after this."

Sara walked over and sat down at the table. Nat pulled his chair close to hers. Too close. Sara took a deep breath, steeling herself for a new onslaught of unwelcome emotions. Neither of them had mentioned the near kiss, but it hung between them, adding a new level of untenable tension to their precarious nonrelationship.

Nat opened a large brown envelope and took out a stack of black-and-white photographs that looked as if they'd been downloaded from the Internet and printed. There were at least half a dozen, all clipped together neatly.

"Where did you get those?"

"From a friend with the FBI. He overnighted them last night, and I got them this morning."

"So that's what Mackie was raising such a ruckus about?"

"Yeah. He doesn't let a vehicle on the property without making sure I know about it."

"That's nice to know. So who are the people in the photographs?"

"They were all connected to Meyers Bickham during the time you lived there. I've arranged them according to the position they held, starting with the caretakers and working up the chain of command. We'll take them one at time and see what, if anything, you can remember about them. Say whatever pops into your mind. Sometimes it's the smallest, most trivial detail that provides the best lead."

Sara was certain that was the most Nat had said at one time since she'd met him. He was apparently taking the bodyguard bit very seriously.

"How did you persuade the FBI to furnish you with these names?"

"Meyers Bickham was a state-owned facility, even though it was managed by a private group. The names of its employees are all public record. The first one is Martha Taylor," he said, sliding a photo in front of her. "She was a caretaker when you arrived. She worked there for three years."

"Are the names of all the residents public record as well?"

"Yes, and the dates they were admitted and released to foster care, adoption, another agency or turned eighteen."

"And what about those of us who just walked off. Does it list us as AWOL?"

"The records indicate you were there until you graduated from high school at age eighteen."

Now why didn't that surprise her? "The records are wrong. I stepped on the school bus the day I turned fifteen and never returned."

"Where did you go?"

"To class for about an hour. Then I walked off

campus and over to the highway. I hitched a ride all the way to Atlanta.''

"How long were you away?"

"Forever. When you escape hell, you don't go back to see if the place has cooled off."

"That's a pretty big record-keeping error."

"That's Meyers Bickham. They probably never even knew I was missing—except maybe when I didn't show up for clean-up duties."

"You were a minor. They should have reported you as a missing person."

"They probably figured I'd wander back in eventually, when the money I'd stolen from the cash box in the office ran out."

"You stole money?"

"Twenty dollars. But the guilt got to me. I mailed it back to them about three years later."

Nat scribbled down some notes. She saw the asterisk he put next to the sentence about the screwed-up records and a series of question marks he'd made in red ink.

"It would be interesting to see what's in your high school records," he said. "They had to give the school some reason for your dropping out in the middle of the year."

"Would that be public record, too?"

"At least records available to you."

"I can call them and see."

"Better to handle it in person."

She groaned as the dread swelled again. "I really don't want to go back there, Nat. It's too close to Meyers Bickham, too close to… Too close to all the things I never want to think about again."

"I know. Believe me, I know." He exhaled

sharply and tapped the photograph. "Martha Tucker. Take a good look and try to place her."

And the journey into misery began again.

NAT TRIED to concentrate on the insect traps he was putting out. Some pests could be eliminated by an organized and timely trapping system, but the traps he was putting out today were only to obtain samples and find out what insects he was dealing with. Once he did, he'd decide how best to control the damage.

Once he knew what he was dealing with.

Which is exactly where he was with the Meyers Bickham investigation. As it was, there wasn't even proof that the basement burial of the babies was associated to any kind of criminal act. But if it wasn't, the threats to Sara so many years after the fact wouldn't make any sense at all.

He'd counted on something clicking this morning when they'd gone over the names and pictures. Nothing had, but then she'd probably worked hard to bury her memories of living in the orphanage.

Only she hadn't actually forgotten. Just mention the place and she turned somber. Unlike now, when he could hear her laughter wafting over from the swimming hole. The day was already a scorcher. He could use a swim himself. Of course, he didn't have a suit. Hadn't needed one before.

But Sara did. She had a black one. He'd seen it drying on the clothesline behind his house yesterday. One piece. Not one of those thong things, but still, it couldn't cover much. Would probably ride up her buttocks when she walked.

And she had a nice butt. Nice legs, too. Great hair. And a terrific smile. Not a bit of pretension about her. She just oozed that well-scrubbed, girl-next-door charm that he'd never expected to be such a turn-on.

His body got into the game, growing hard and making his jeans feel as if they'd shrunk two sizes in the wash. He worked another fifteen minutes, then gave up and walked toward the swimming hole.

He'd been a recluse for three years, had feared he might never have any kind of normal, red-blooded interest in a woman again. Now he couldn't even stay away from Sara long enough to get a few chores done.

But he had to be cautious. He was just starting to claw his way back from what he'd thought had been a bottomless pit. He wasn't doing anything to risk slipping and plummeting to the bottom again. Especially now, when he needed all his wits about him to make sure Sara and Kendra stayed safe.

Reverie set in and his mind slipped back to that heartbreaking night. Back to Maria, with her shiny black hair and midnight eyes. Back to her daughter, young and carefree, laughing and tugging at his hand to get his attention the way Kendra did.

The pain hit again, socked him in the gut with the force of a boxer's right fist and Nat felt as if the walls of his chest were caving in on him.

The ending might have been different if he hadn't overstepped the boundaries, if he hadn't missed all the danger signs. It was a mistake he would never make again.

"THROW ME AGAIN, Mommy."

Sara lifted Kendra and tossed her into the cool water. Kendra splashed and came up giggling.

"Do it again. Do it again."

"One more time. Then I have to take a break before my arms fall off."

"Your arms won't fall off."

"You're right, but they'll ache so much I won't be able to make chocolate chip cookies tonight."

"Okay, one more time."

Sara lifted her again, gave her a toss and watched until she surfaced again. "Come and catch me," she called to Kendra, swimming toward the bank.

Kendra swam after her, her strokes even and quite skilled for a four-year-old. Of course she'd been swimming in the apartment pool since she was two. Mackie, who'd already had his swim and had been watching them from the bank, jumped into the water to meet them.

When Sara waded onto the bank, she looked up and saw Nat watching them. He was sitting under a hickory tree, leaning back on his hands, his legs spread out in front of him. She bent and retrieved the towel she'd left on the grass, then tugged her bathing suit, making sure it fully covered her bottom.

"I don't want to get out yet," Kendra said, pulling her lips into a childish pout.

"You can stay on the edge, but don't go in the deep water."

"I can swim, Mommy."

"I know you can, but you still have to stay in the shallow water or else get out."

"But—"

"No buts."

"Okay, Mommy. I'll stay right here."

"Thata girl."

Sara dried her hair with the towel, certain that it

looked a frizzled fright. Not that she'd look like a bathing beauty had her hair been perfect.

Nat was in his usual uniform, faded jeans and a sport shirt, open at the neck and with the sleeves rolled up to just under his elbows. But he'd shed his shoes and socks and he'd thrown his Braves baseball cap on the grass beside him.

She noticed again how much the haircut had changed his appearance, made him look younger, but still rugged. Not that he didn't still have plenty of hair.

"How long have you had the beard?" she asked, as she spread the towel and sat down beside him.

"Where did that question come from?"

"I was just wondering how you'd look without it."

"I haven't shaved since I bought the orchard."

"Three year's growth. No wonder it looks thick enough birds could nest in it."

"Just small birds."

"Isn't a beard hot in these Georgia summers?"

"Everything's hot in Georgia summers."

"Then why don't you shave it off?" *Or I could do it for you.* Fortunately she stopped herself before she blurted that out. The haircut had almost done her in. What would shaving him do to her libido—or to his?

They sat there, the silence awkward. It was the nature of their fragile friendship, she decided. They'd skipped too many steps, jumped from strangers to housemates. No wonder neither of them had been ready for the hot arousal that had accompanied last night's haircut and lingered as a slow burn today.

Kendra waded onto the bank and over to where they were sitting, Mackie following right behind her. "Hi, Mr. Nat. Do you wanna swim with me?"

"I don't have a bathing suit."

"Go get yours."

"I don't have one to get."

"We can buy you one, can't we, Mommy?"

"We can and I think we should. After all, we took over his swimming hole."

"You come back and swim with me, Mommy."

"I will in a minute. Do you want some juice or some peanut butter crackers?"

"Not yet." And then she was gone again, she and Mackie running back to the water's edge.

Nat ran his fingers through his hair, probably from habit now that it no longer fell into his face. "You're really good with Kendra. She's spirited, but she minds well and the two of you really have fun together."

"She's pretty much my life. Plus I guess I try to make up for the fact that she doesn't see much of her father."

"Where is he?"

"In New Hampshire."

"That's a long way from Georgia."

"He took a job coaching basketball for a college up there right after the divorce. He's supposed to get Kendra for Thanksgiving week and for a month in the summer, but he's getting married this summer—in England."

"So he just gave up his month with his daughter?"

"He didn't seem to see it as a big deal."

"Does he know about the threats?"

"I told him. He thinks I'm paranoid. What about you, Nat? Were you ever married?"

"No."

Back to his one-word responses—about the most

she ever got from him when the conversation turned to anything about his personal life. It was as if he had some kind of radar that shot up instant barriers whenever anyone attempted to reach the real Nat Sanderson.

She lay on her towel, at an angle that allowed her to keep an eye on Kendra. But she wasn't ready to give up trying to get to know Nat better. "What were you like growing up?"

"A typical boy. I liked riding my bike and playing sports. Hated school and homework."

"Did you have brothers and sisters?"

"No, I was an only child."

"Where are your parents now?"

"You ask a lot of questions."

"And every now and then you slip up and answer one or two."

"My parents are alive and well and living in Austin, Texas. Yes, I'm a Texan and no, I'm not a cowboy. We lived in town." He stood. "Now I need to get back to work."

"You don't have to. The inquisition's over. I'm going back to swim with Kendra."

She walked off before he did. That gave her a small level of satisfaction. Except that she had to turn back and ask him one more question—this one not personal.

"Do you need anything from the store? I need to drive to Mattie's and pick up some fresh tomatoes and squash for dinner. You do eat squash, don't you?"

"Not knowingly."

"It's good for you."

"So *that's* what's wrong with it."

"And I need to drive back to the cabin. I forgot to pack an extra bottle of Kendra's vitamins and she's about out."

"Give me another hour to finish up in the orchard and I'll go with you."

"I'm sure we'll be fine on our own to drive down the road."

"Wait for me."

His tone had grown stern, as if he were issuing an order that she'd best follow. It grated on her. Nothing could rile her faster than having someone bark an order at her. No doubt a holdover from the senseless rules and constant barking of orders she'd endured at Meyers Bickham.

"I just don't want you going back to the cabin by yourself," Nat said. "Just a precaution, but it will make me feel better."

His tone was much friendlier, meaning he'd evidently read her reaction and understood. "I'll wait," she said as her irritation dissolved into a rush of warmth that he not only didn't think her paranoid but wanted to protect her.

She hurried to join Kendra at the bank before she did something foolish like walk back to where Nat was standing. One look into his dark, compelling eyes right now and who knew what she might do.

The first step into the water was the eye-opener. The cold seemed to jump inside her, rushing from her feet to her head, and tingling along every nerve. Exactly what she needed.

"Look at that cloud, Mommy. It's very black."

Sara looked in the direction Kendra was pointing. Black smoke billowed into the air as if from a giant chimney. It was north of them, but she couldn't tell how far. Possibly in the far end of the orchard or in the woods beyond.

"Nat! Wait!"

"What is it?"

"A fire." She pointed toward the cloud. "Is it on your property?"

"It's north of the orchard."

"North of the orchard. That would put it close to the cabin."

"In that area."

"We have to check it out." She splashed into the water and grabbed Kendra. Nat grabbed her towel and the small cooler of snacks and juice she'd brought with her to the swimming hole.

"Get your keys," he said when they reached the house. "I'll buckle Kendra into her seat."

She did as he said, then tossed him the keys. He knew a lot more about the area than she did. She'd leave the driving to him.

Sara tried to remember what she'd left in the cabin as the van climbed the mountain road. Towels and linens, some clothes and food staples, cleaning supplies and books. None of which she wanted to lose, but the cabin had stood in that same place for fifty years. There was no reason to think it had suddenly caught fire on a brilliant summer day when it wasn't even inhabited.

No reason at all.

A DOZEN POSSIBILITIES stalked Nat's mind as he drove the last mile to the Jackson cabin, the air growing thick with the pungent odor of burning wood. He'd reserve final judgment until he saw evidence, but he had a strong suspicion that the threats toward

Sara and Kendra had just jumped to a whole new level.

And he just might be the reason behind that jump.

He skidded to a stop at the end of the road. Sara jumped out of the van before it came to a full stop. By the time the engine died, she was already running down the path to the footbridge.

He took off after her, but before he could reach her he heard her scream, a terrified scream that tore at his insides. A scream that sounded as if she'd come to face-to-face with the devil himself.

Chapter Eight

Sara was standing on the footbridge, ghostly white, and as stiff as if she were carved from ice. She held a baby doll in her outstretched hands. Only the doll's head was missing and in its place was a hideous skull.

The doll slipped from her hands just as Nat reached her and the limp toy body fell into the water. The skull hit the railing and fell onto the bridge, bouncing across as if it were alive.

Nat pulled Sara into his arms and held her close, cradling the back of her head in his hand and crooning meaningless reassurances.

"It's okay, Sara. It's okay."

She held on to him, clinging, and he felt her tears wet and roll down his cheeks to the backdrop of crashing timbers and the heat of the roaring fire. The situation had grown from merely frightening to macabre, from idle threats to venomous ferocity.

And still he was all too keenly aware of Sara's lithe body pressed against his. He trembled at the warmth of her breath on his neck and the dampness of her hair in his hands—and the fact that she was still dressed in the black bathing suit.

"Mommy! Mommy!"

Sara jerked from his grasp. For a second he'd forgotten all about Kendra, but when he turned she was running toward them, not even slowing as she propelled herself into Sara's arms.

"The pictures I painted you are getting burned up!"

Sara rocked Kendra in her arms the way he had done her just seconds before. "I'm sorry, sweetie, but the fire is too dangerous. We can't go into the cabin."

"But my Beanie Babies are in there, too."

Kendra started to cry, and Nat seethed with anger. He'd love to get his hands on the sick bastard who'd done this. "We'll get new beanie things," Nat said, having no idea what they were.

"But I like mine."

"I know you do," Sara said. Her voice was unsteady, but she wore the expression of a hardened general facing his troops in the heat of battle. "But you'll like the new ones, too." Her gaze went to the skull. "I think we should take that with us, Nat, to show to the sheriff."

"I'll take care of it. Why don't you take Kendra back to the van. When you get there, call 9-1-1 and report the fire. The rangers will likely send a fire-fighting team down to keep this from becoming a major forest fire."

"It's arson," she said, her voice cracking on the word as if it pained her even to say it. "Whoever planted the doll for me to find set the fire."

He only nodded, certain she was right. "No one's hurt. Everything else can be replaced."

She set Kendra back on the bridge, then led her

up the path toward the van. Nat watched them walk away, his insides so tight he felt as if he might explode at any second. There probably wasn't a way in the world he could have stopped this, but still it grated on him that some depraved psycho with dirty secrets to hide was able to wreak such havoc.

Sara didn't deserve this and Kendra certainly didn't.

Nat walked over and picked up the skull. It wasn't even real, just a cheap plastic imitation, probably from some kid's science kit or maybe even a Halloween decoration. There were strips of adhesive tape over the hole for the mouth, no doubt a visual representation of the threat that Sara was not to tell anything she knew about whatever depravity had occurred at Meyers Bickham.

The skull might be a cheap imitation, but the fire was real. And the message. Whatever had happened at Meyers Bickham all those years ago was deadly serious, and some psycho would go to any lengths to keep Sara quiet.

Nat watched the back part of the cabin roof fall in, heard the crash and the clatter and felt the eruption of heat on his skin.

And he knew at that moment that the apples were forgotten. He wasn't the man he'd been before the fatal night that had sent him running from life three and a half years ago, but his days of shunning reality and any feelings other than regret were over.

Look out, you sonofabitch. 'Cause I'm coming to get you, and this time I won't make any mistakes.

THE MAN STOOD in the shadows of the forest and turned his high-powered binoculars from Sara Murdoch to the bearded mountain man who'd wormed his way so quickly into her life. If he'd been looking at the man through the scope of his rifle instead of the binoculars, he could have picked him off in a heartbeat. One pull of the trigger and the man would become history.

But Nat Sanderson wasn't his concern. His job was to make certain Sara kept her mouth shut. Frankly he wasn't convinced she remembered anything. But if it came back to her, she'd tell.

Little Sara Thomas, at least that had been her name back then, the bratty redhead with an attitude. She'd been that way as a kid and from what he could tell, she hadn't changed much. If it had been up to him, she'd have been buried in the same musty graves as the unfortunate babies.

And if she continued to ignore his warnings, if she kept telling her story to sheriffs or anyone else— well, he'd do what he had to. And if he enjoyed the act, so much the better.

He watched Nat Sanderson pick up the skull and examine it. Nothing but a cheap plastic imitation, but it had worked. Sara had gone berserk when she'd seen it. And Sanderson had run to her rescue, had probably gotten all hot and bothered by the near-naked woman in his arms. A recluse like him probably hadn't even known what a woman felt like before that.

Leave it to Sara to go running to some stupid apple farmer for protection. For a college professor, the woman was downright dumb.

THEY'D BEEN BACK at Nat's rambling farmhouse for an hour and Sara was still shaken, though she'd managed to calm Kendra with a couple of stories and a board game. Kendra was outside with Mackie again now, tossing a stick that the lab fetched every time, as if his retrieving it were a marvelous feat.

Sara had seen little of Nat since they'd returned. He'd been comforting and reassuring at the scene, but he'd withdrawn on the way back to the house, slid behind that wall of silence that he could erect at a moment's notice.

She was certain this was more than he'd bargained for. He'd expected them to stay at his house for a few days and then move back into the cabin. Now there was no cabin to go back to.

But it made the decision-making easy. She couldn't expect to spend the summer with Nat. She'd simply have to drive back to Columbus. Nat would tell her she didn't have to leave, but he'd probably be relieved that they were going.

She poured herself a glass of lemonade and walked out the back door. She might as well find Nat and let him know she and Kendra would be leaving in the morning, though she hadn't told Kendra yet.

"Have you seen Mr. Nat?" she asked as Kendra ran by, chasing Mackie who was chasing a rabbit who'd made the bad decision to hop into the open.

"He's in the apple shed. He told me to tell you if you came outside."

The shed was only a few yards behind the house. There were no apples in there now, but there were bushel baskets and equipment for making apple cider and lots of tools, only about half of which Sara had ever seen before. The shed consisted of two units. The side where the tools were kept was enclosed.

The other part didn't have a fourth wall and appeared to be used for packing.

Sara had wandered into the shed the first night she'd spent at the house. Nat had found her there and had answered her questions. Apples were the one part of his life he didn't seem to mind talking about.

But it wasn't apples she was interested in this afternoon. She stepped into the open area. It was nearing six, but there was still more than enough daylight to illuminate the shed. The waning rays glistened off the bottom of a copper tub that hung on the wall and skirted the shadows cast by the handscrew press.

Nat was nowhere to be seen, but the narrow door to the enclosed part of the shed was ajar. She knocked and waited.

"Door's open. Come on in."

Nat was leaning over a worktable that ran the length of the shed. He didn't look up, just kept his eyes on the pistol he was cleaning. A rifle and another pistol were also on the table. The sight of the small arsenal of weapons set off a new spiral of dread.

"What are you doing?"

"Cleaning my guns."

"But why?"

"They haven't been used in a while."

"And there's no reason to use them now, Nat."

"I'm not the one making the rules of engagement."

"No, some lunatic is, but we can't sink to his level."

"If it is a 'he' behind this," Nat corrected. "We don't actually know that. Most of the caretakers at the orphanage were women."

"My caller the other night was a man. Besides, I just can't see a woman doing something as gruesome as replacing a doll's head with a skull."

"Some women are capable of far more grisly deeds than that."

"I guess." She pulled up a metal stool and hoisted herself onto it. "If this made any sense at all, it would be easier to deal with, but it doesn't. I heeded the threats. I kept silent. So why did someone burn down the cabin that didn't even belong to me?"

"You talked to the sheriff in charge of the case. Maybe the psycho thinks you told him something."

"But how would anyone except Sheriff Wesley and other law enforcement people know that? For that matter, how did anyone even know to look for me in this area, or in a cabin that was at the end of a washed-out road?"

"Someone did, and that's what worries me." He held the pistol up, squinted and stared down the chamber. "I don't think we should tell the sheriff about the fire. We'll just leave sheriffs and any other cops out of this for a while."

"Won't I need a police report, in case the cabin was insured?"

"Things move slowly up here. A few day's delay in reporting the fire won't matter much one way or the other."

"I don't plan to be here a few days longer."

Nat turned and stared at her, unspoken questions swimming in his dark eyes. She slid from the stool, walked over and put a hand to his shoulder. The awareness level zinged through her, but she let the hand stay. "Kendra and I will be leaving in the morning."

His gaze returned to the weapon he was cleaning, but she didn't miss the tightening of his muscles or the taut pull to his lips.

"The danger's not going to dissolve just because you go back to your apartment in Columbus, Sara."

Sara shuddered, wishing he were wrong, but fearing he was right. Her gaze fell to the guns and she felt as if she were caught up in some bizarre video game and that the guns might jump up at any second and start firing in random directions.

Only she wasn't in a game, and the guns wouldn't fire themselves. If they fired shots, they would be in Nat's hands—and the killings would be on her conscience.

"I can't stay here, Nat. I can't do this to you. You're an apple grower. You're not a gunfighter."

He exhaled sharply, then aimed the pistol at some invisible target. "You're wrong, Sara. That's exactly what I am—or what I was."

NAT FELT Sara's gaze boring into him, could almost feel the change in their relationship as his words sank in. To her credit, she didn't just turn tail and run, but he felt as if she were slinking away from him even though her feet were not moving.

"Who are you? What are you?" Her voice was strained, but forceful. "If I'm going to trust you, I have a right to know."

The old, familiar memories swelled inside him until they seemed to cut off the blood supply to his brain. "Let's get out of here. Take a walk down to the orchard."

"I can't leave Kendra."

"She can go with us."

"I'm not sure I want her to hear this."

"She'll run and play with Mackie and pay no attention to us or our conversation."

Sara nodded, but the agreement was almost defiant. He understood. She'd been through a lot this week and had no real reason to trust him, especially now.

A slight breeze picked up the tendrils of Sara's hair and tossed them into her face as she went to lure Kendra from a hole she was digging near the back steps.

He waited until Kendra and Sara joined them, then started the short walk to the orchard where the Jonagolds grew and where Blake had mowed recently enough to make the walk easy for Kendra and Sara.

Apples had been his salvation over the past few years and growing them organically had seemed somehow good for his soul. Now they seemed to have lost any power to soothe or comfort.

It was as if the fire and the cruelty of the skull-topped doll had released some kind of toxic chemicals into his system. They stirred the old emotions, brought back the edgy strain and the adrenaline loads that used to rule his life.

Only if he was honest, he'd have to admit the old ways had been riding the surface ever since the first time Sara had told him about the threats and he'd seen the fear in her eyes.

As he predicted, Kendra ran ahead of them, skipping along behind Mackie and stopping to pick up and toss an occasional bad apple that had fallen from the tree. He waited for Sara's questions to start as his mind darted from the past to the present, as if there were some electrical current that ran between the two.

"You weren't some kind of paid assassin, were you?"

"No, nothing like that."

"Thank God."

Relief flooded her voice, and he decided it was probably best not to admit that at one time he'd considered that option.

"So what were you?"

"I started out as a cop. Then I worked for the FBI."

"Why did you leave?"

"My assignments weren't as exciting as I'd imagined." Not even close. Not back then, when he'd lived for the highs that danger provided. "I would have worked into the more exciting assignments but I was young and didn't want to wait."

"So you moved to Georgia and started growing apples? I don't buy that for a minute."

"I'd have been disappointed if you had. When I left the Bureau, I went to work for a friend who runs a private security business for high-profile people."

"Like movie stars?"

"Entertainers, politicians, foreign diplomats. Anyone with big bucks who's willing to pay top dollar for protection."

"So you actually were a bodyguard?"

"That's about the size of it."

"And that was exciting enough for you?"

"Some of the time."

She stopped walking and leaned against the trunk of a tree, propping the sole of one foot against it.

"That still doesn't explain why you're in Georgia. Apple trees don't need a bodyguard."

He swallowed hard, the memories so potent he feared they might engulf him the way the fire had consumed the cabin this afternoon, just pull him back inside and finish destroying him. And all of them began and ended with a woman with coal-black hair and light brown skin. A woman with...

"I made mistakes," he said, forcing the words past an ache that just wouldn't quit. "I guess I came here to look for a way to live with them."

"So what am I, Nat? A way of paying your dues? Save the scared woman and her kid, and all your mistakes are justified?"

"You might have been—in the beginning," he admitted, knowing she was too smart to fool with lies.

"And now?"

He took her hands in his. Feelings bucked around inside him. The kind of feelings he didn't need. The kind that had messed him up before. "You're in danger, Sara. You and Kendra. I wouldn't be much of a man if I didn't do what I can to help."

"And that's the only reason you want to help us?"

He looked into her eyes, saw the questioning and the fear, but he saw something there that bothered him even more. He saw the same desire that burned inside him.

"Do the reasons really matter? I'm offering my services as a bodyguard and as a former FBI agent and cop. I'll protect you and try to get to the bottom of the threats. You don't have a hell of a lot of other choices, the way I see it. And running back to Columbus damn sure isn't an answer."

She grimaced, her lips pulled taut. "Okay, Nat. We'll stay, at least for now."

"Good."

Because there wasn't a way in the world he would have let her walk away without him. Not until he knew she was safe. He dropped her hands and stepped away before he gave in to his hunger for her and took her in his arms beneath the spreading shade of an apple tree.

NAT STOOD in front of the bathroom mirror, holding the straight razor and considering if he really wanted to lather up and shave away the hair that defined the reclusive apple grower he'd become. It was a mask of sorts, something to hide behind. He'd had it for so long, he wasn't sure he'd even recognize the face beneath the mask.

But Sara was right. The beard was hot in the summer. And the beard seemed more in keeping with growing apples than it did with investigating a case involving the burial of babies without identities. When he was investigating or protecting, he sometimes liked to go unnoticed, and that wouldn't happen with the kind of beard that birds could nest in.

So, ready or not, the beard had to go. He took the top from a can of shaving cream he'd had on hand for months and sprayed mounds of white foam into his hand. Then he worked the cream into the roots of the beard and got the straight razor ready.

He'd never really used one before, and didn't relish the idea of having the sharp blade so close to his neck. But, other than his scythe, a really sharp straight razor might be the only thing that could mow through the thick growth.

Reluctantly, knowing that once he'd started, there would be no going back, he made the first swipe. The blade scraped his flesh and wooly clumps of hair slid from his face, down his bare chest and into the sink.

"MOMMY, can I watch *Beauty and the Beast?*"

Sara glanced at her watch. "It's too near bedtime to see the whole thing but you can watch part of it if you like."

"Will you watch it with me?"

"Okay." It beat sitting around thinking of the burning cabin and the beheaded doll. There were beasts, and then there were beasts. The type that found some perverse pleasure in torturing her when she'd done nothing. And the type in the movie, with a real heart beneath the bravado and appearance.

The kind like Nat—who disguised himself so well, she wasn't sure even he knew who he was anymore. One thing was clear. The mistakes he'd made—whatever they'd been—called all the shots. They'd chased him from a life of danger and risk to one of solitude and physical toil. But not one of true happiness.

What his words didn't say, his eyes did. And there was a dark and brooding timbre to them that seemed to mirror the anguish that lived somewhere inside him.

A man of mystery and intrigue. Quiet, but strong. Seemingly simple, but totally complex. Rough around the edges, yet masculine and virile. She sighed. No wonder the guy affected her like none she'd met before.

"Do you think Mr. Nat wants to watch the movie with us?"

"I doubt it, sweetheart."

"I'll ask him." Kendra went skipping down the hall, calling for Nat. She wasn't particularly loud, but her voice echoed through the house. A second later it changed to a scream.

Sara took off running, heart pounding. She stopped at the bathroom door, then grabbed hold of the facing for support as a different kind of jolt from the one she'd expected shot through her.

Nat was standing in front of the mirror, half his face shaved, a trickle of blood dripping off his exposed chin.

"It's just a tiny cut, Kendra. Like a skinned knee. Doesn't even hurt."

"But your face is bleeding off your whiskers!"

"They're not bleeding off. I'm shaving them off. See." He held up the straight razor and finally noticed Sara. "Sorry. Guess I forgot to lock the door. Kendra burst in, saw the blood and thought I'd hurt myself."

Sara tried to answer, may have even moved her mouth, but nothing came out. He still had on his faded jeans, unsnapped, but he was barefooted and bare-chested and...

And she had to stop staring.

"You did cut yourself," she said, finally managing to swallow and force the words past the lump in her throat.

"Just a scratch."

Sara wet the edge of a clean washcloth and dabbed at the drops of blood.

"It's okay," Nat whispered.

He grabbed her wrist but it was his eyes that held

her. More than dark and brooding now. They were inviting. Seducing. Mesmerizing.

"C'mon, Mommy, let's go watch the movie," Kendra announced.

The spell broke, or at least loosened enough that Sara could breathe. "You go ahead, sweetheart."

"But you said you'd watch it with me."

"I know. You go ahead and start it. I'll join you in a bit."

"I'm glad it doesn't hurt when your beard falls off," Kendra said, then skipped back down the hall to her movie leaving Nat and Sara alone.

Nat started to shave again, and Sara stared openly, unable to take her eyes from him. Her gaze moved from his face, over his muscled chest, to the bulge inside his jeans.

"You're going to miss the movie," Nat said, his voice hoarse as if they'd been making love.

"I've seen it," she said, stepping closer. "Why don't you let me finish that for you."

"I've never trusted a woman at my throat with a straight razor before."

"But you said you liked risk and danger."

"Did I say that?"

"That's what I heard." She trailed her fingers from his left earlobe all the way down his back. "Go sit in the kitchen, Nat. I'll bring the razor and a bowl of warm water."

"Are you sure you want to do this?"

"Very sure."

She watched him walk away, thinking she'd probably lost her mind and not really caring. She was lost in the need to touch Nat and feel the roughened skin of his face and neck as the whiskers fell away.

Wanted to feel something besides dread and fear and the horrors of Meyers Bickham slipping back into her life.

She joined Nat in the kitchen. Even the warm water, slick with shaving cream, felt like some exotic aphrodisiac as she rinsed the razor, then gingerly touched it to Nat's neck. She brought it upward, firm and steady strokes in spite of the fact that her stomach was fluttering and her heart seemed to be stuck somewhere around her throat.

The simple act of touching and raking the blade through the thick growth of hair was more erotic than Sara could have imagined. Desire ran hot inside her and pooled down deep as she cut the remaining clusters of coarse hair from his face.

She rinsed the razor a last time, then wet a cloth in the hot water and sponged his face. She let her fingers linger on his flesh, relishing the texture of his chin and the lines and angles of his jaw.

"All done," she said, removing the warm cloth from his face. "Want to see the results?"

Her answer was Nat's hands pulling her into his lap. And then his lips were on hers and the desire that had run hot in her blood for the past ten minutes exploded inside her.

The kiss was raw hunger, a kind of savage need that shook Sara clear through to her soul. She kissed Nat back, over and over, sliding her tongue into his mouth and parrying with his. She simply couldn't get enough of the taste or the feel of him.

She was so lost in the kisses, lost in Nat, that the shrill ringing seemed part of the moment until Nat pulled away.

"You should probably answer that."

"My phone."

"Yeah. You don't have to answer it, but..."

But with all that was going on, she couldn't very well ignore it. She walked across the room and picked it up from the counter where she'd left it. "Hello."

"Is this Sara Murdoch who resides in the Hillside Apartments?"

"Yes."

"This is Lieutenant Buzz Fontaine with the Columbus Police Department."

"Is something wrong?"

"Yes, ma'am. I'm afraid I have some really bad news for you. There's been a break-in at your apartment, and an assault."

"Raye Ann?"

"Yes, ma'am."

"Is she okay?"

"No, ma'am. She's not."

Sara started to shake and the phone slipped from her fingers and crashed against the cold hard floor.

Chapter Nine

Nat steadied Sara, then grabbed the phone. After identifying himself, he listened to the account of the attack on Raye Ann Jackson. Someone had broken into Sara's apartment where Raye Ann was staying and was apparently in the act of burglarizing the place when she'd come home that evening. They'd hit her over the head with a blunt, heavy object and fled.

Raye Ann was still unconscious, as she'd been when a neighbor saw the door open and found her lying on the floor just inside the doorway. Her condition was listed as critical.

Sara stood there until he'd finished the conversation, then let him lead her to the front porch. She dropped into the swing, and he sat down beside her. He tried to pull her into the circle of his arm, but she resisted so he just left his arm on the back of the swing.

Sara stared at her clutched hands as she listened to the few details Nat had learned. ''Raye Ann may die and this is all my fault, Nat,'' she said, the second he'd gotten the last word out of his mouth. ''I was trying to do something nice for her by letting her use the apartment and it may have gotten her killed.''

"The lieutenant said burglary was the probable motive.''

"There's never been a problem with break-ins in that building. I don't know why or how, but this is connected to the threats and Meyers Bickham. I'm sure of it.''

He wouldn't argue with Sara when she was lost in the throes of grief and guilt. Besides, he had a feeling she was right, though it didn't add up at this point. Why Raye Ann? And why bother with Sara's apartment when whoever was threatening Sara knew she was in North Georgia?

Or maybe they didn't. The guy may not have known she'd moved in with Nat and thought she'd gone back to her apartment when the cabin burned down. But if he knew she'd talked to Sheriff Wesley, then he surely knew she'd done it at Nat's house.

"Raye Ann is a good person, Nat. She's only in her mid-sixties and still teaching. She's had a hard time after her husband's fatal heart attack, but she was moving ahead in spite of it, even remodeling her house. Now…''

What could he say? Nothing that changed anything. "She may pull through.''

"But she's still unconscious and on the critical list. That doesn't sound too promising.''

"You can call the hospital and check for yourself. Maybe there's been a change for the better.''

"If only she hadn't been staying in my apartment, if I hadn't come…'' Sara stopped midsentence, reached over and gripped his hand. "If I'd gone back there with Kendra, she could have been—'' Her voice broke.

"Don't do this, Sara. Kendra wasn't there. She's here with us and she's safe."

"Safe for now. But this won't stop. That's the way it's always been with Meyers Bickham. Every time I think I've put it behind me, it jumps up and bites me again. I truly hate that place."

"Do you want to talk about it?"

She stiffened as if her blood had suddenly turned to hardened cement. "It was just an old building where kids with nowhere to go lived."

"Then why do you hate it so much?"

"Because... Because... Because I was so alone there."

Pent-up emotion, the shock and grief of what had happened to Raye Ann, and the fears and terrors of the past few days seemed to all hit her at once.

Sobs shook her body and tears ran down her face, but this time when Nat pulled her into his arms, she didn't resist. He cradled her against him and felt her tears on his neck.

He couldn't explain his feelings for Sara any more than he could explain the sweetness of his apples or the way the redbirds found their way back to his orchards year after year. All he knew was that it almost killed him to see her like this. And that he'd do anything in his power to keep her safe. Anything.

Finally her sobs weakened to sniffling. He took a clean handkerchief from his back pocket and handed it to her. She blew her nose, sniffed a few more times, then pulled from his arms again. "I didn't mean to break down like that."

"You were entitled."

"I can't go on like this, Nat. Just waiting for the next horror. Keeping quiet is obviously not enough. I have to do something. Have to find some way to fight back."

"Now you're talking."

"Talking your language, but it's so foreign to me. I think I've always taken the path of least resistance."

"You? A woman who grew up in an orphanage, set out on her own at fifteen and is now a college history professor? I'd say you've been a fighter all your life."

"But not with guns blaring and a backdrop of muscle and brawn. I just go after what I want and ignore what I don't want to deal with, the way I've forgotten most of what it was like to grow up in Meyers Bickham, the way I pretended my marriage to Steven was working when it was falling apart at the seams. The way I would be forgetting the threats now if they hadn't escalated to the point where I have to deal with them."

"But you do what you have to in order to survive and make a good life for yourself and Kendra. That takes the ultimate courage, Sara, far more than just shooting it out with the enemy. That's why men go to war and women keep love and goodness and hope alive. It's us who take the easier route."

"I'm going to war now, Nat. So tell me what to do."

"I think we should start by going back to your high school and finding out exactly what's in your records. Then we need to make a return visit to Sheriff Troy Wesley and level with him as to what's gone on here—and hope he'll trust us enough to level with us.''

''See the sheriff again and wait to see who gets hurt next, or at the very least what gets burned down or destroyed?''

''Either you're ready to fight this thing or you're not, Sara. There's no such thing as a peaceful war.''

''When do you want to make this trip?''

''Tomorrow. It's not that long a drive. We'll take Highway 52 West.''

She stretched her legs in front of her, stopping the gentle sway of the swing. ''Tomorrow?''

''There's no reason to put it off.''

''I know. I just wish Steven had taken Kendra out of all of this. I don't want to frighten her, but if she's with us, she'll pick up on the fact that something dangerous is going on.''

''I think we should leave her with Dorinda.''

''I can't leave her with a stranger. I can't leave her at all, not with all that's going on.''

''She'll be safe. I'll talk to Henry, make sure he stays around to keep an eye on things.''

''He's a farmer, Nat. He's not prepared to deal with the kind of psycho we're dealing with.''

''He's an ex-Green Beret. He's probably the one man in the whole area who can deal with it.''

''So you weren't the total recluse you seemed.''

''Henry helped me get the apple orchard started. His dad had an orchard when he was growing up. We talked some. Men talk.''

''About killing.''

''Sometimes.''

She exhaled slowly, then stood. ''Okay, Nat. I can't just sit here any longer and do nothing. We'll go to the Callahan farm and talk to Dorinda in the morning. If I feel comfortable with the situation, we'll drive to my old high school and then make a call on the sheriff.''

"Good." It was a start, but there was more. He hated to lay it on her tonight, but it had to be done. "There is something else you can do, Sara."

"What's that?"

"You have to try and remember details about your life at the orphanage, especially anything to do with that basement. I'd like you to make notes of anything that comes to mind."

Nat saw the change in her immediately. It was as if he'd ripped her newfound resolve away and replaced it with something dark and sinister.

"I'll try."

"And if you need me tonight, I'll be right down the hall." It was an offer he'd never expected to be making and one he wasn't certain he could fulfill. He didn't know what he actually had left emotionally.

Up until this week, he'd thought there was nothing there. That had changed, but still, he wasn't sure that when it came right down to it he'd have enough of himself left to give a woman like Sara what she needed.

He had to be very careful from this point on. Emotions got in the way of protecting, and that was the main thing Sara needed from him. The one thing he was determined to give.

SARA STOOD at the window of the guest bedroom where she slept, staring out and thinking how she dreaded going back to the high school she'd attended while at Meyers Bickham. There were no good memories there.

"Are you okay?"

She turned to find Nat standing at the door, a cup of something hot and steamy in hand.

"Not particularly."

"I knocked but you must not have heard me."

"I wasn't here. I was lost in the past."

"I made hot chocolate. I thought you might like a cup."

"Thanks." She walked over and took it from his hand, spying the melted marshmallows floating on top. "You went all out."

"I thought you might need a comfort drink."

"You never cease to surprise me."

"I've surprised myself these last few days."

She sipped the chocolate slowly, letting the warmth seep down her throat. "This doesn't taste like straight chocolate."

"I added a bit of Kahlúa to it."

"To help those old memories shake free?"

"Got to loosen the rusty hinges of your mind."

"I've tried to think about Meyers Bickham. So far I've had difficulty getting past the first day."

"First impressions are sometimes the best place to start."

Sara sat on the edge of the mattress and forced her mind to travel through time. The features coalesced slowly, like shadows in deepening twilight.

"My first impression. The building had originally been a church. It still looked like one from the outside, but once I walked through the wide doors, it seemed cold and frightening, nothing like the church in my old neighborhood had made me feel."

"Did it still have pews?"

"No. There were mostly offices where the pews would have been. And there was one big meeting room and a smaller room where we could go and watch TV occasionally. But we didn't get to control the channels, and no one ever wanted to watch what the caretakers chose for us."

"Where did you sleep?"

"In the back—in small rooms that were lined with bunk beds. We had our own drawers for clothes and personal items. That was about it." Or at least all she could remember.

"What about the basement?"

"Dark. It was dark, and frightening. Down steep stairs." She shivered, suddenly cold and feeling as if she were about to be swallowed up by something that smelled of death.

"How do you know that? You said you'd never been down there."

She shook her head, suddenly nauseous and dizzy. "I don't know. But that's how it was in my nightmares. That's what happens when I try to remember what it was like when I first went there. It's all so tangled in my mind."

"Then how can you be certain you were never in the basement?"

"Because the things I remember can't be real." She started to shake.

Nat crossed the room, sat down on the bed beside her and took her hands in his. "What do you remember?"

"Big gray rats. And ghosts. And a parade."

"Tell me about it."

"You'll think I'm crazy."

"You're not crazy, Sara. You just had a lot to deal with for a little girl. Do you still have the nightmares?"

"Sometimes. Not so often anymore. And they change. But almost always there are the rats. And the parade. And a ghost baby that just keeps crying and crying and crying until I finally wake up in a cold sweat."

"Who's in the parade?"

"That's what is so crazy. I'm not sure who's in the parade. Ghosts, I think. One of them carries a lantern. But sometimes…" She shrank into herself, hating the demons that seemed to live in the dark corners of her mind and come out at times like this to torment her. "Sometimes it's my mother leading the parade."

Nat reached over and brushed locks of errant curls from her face. "Sometimes nightmares are based on actual events that are too disturbing to deal with when you're awake."

"I've thought of that, but they change so much. Sometimes I'm alone. Sometimes I'm with friends who run off and leave me alone with the ghostly parade. And then there's my mother. I know for certain she was never in that basement."

"What happened to your parents?"

"My father died when I was five. He got his sleeve caught in some kind of machinery at the factory where he worked. I never heard the details. I'm sure they were gruesome. Then my mom got cancer. She fought. She fought really hard. But one day the ambulance came and took her to the hospital. She never came home again."

Nat put a hand to the back of his neck and let his

thumb roam the tight tendons below her right earlobe. "You've been through a lot, Sara, and you'll get through this. And you won't have to do it alone. I'll be here every step of the way."

"I'd like to believe that."

"But you don't?"

"No one has ever stuck it out with me before. I have trouble believing you'll be different."

"Then you really don't know me."

"I'm learning."

"Me, too." He let his fingers tangle in her hair. "You've probably done enough thinking for tonight. You should get some sleep."

"I'll try."

He trailed a finger down her cheek, letting it linger on her lips. For a second she thought he might kiss her again, but instead he got up and walked to the door quickly, as if fighting his own emotions—or his own demons. Or maybe he was just rethinking his promise to get involved in trouble that didn't belong to him.

CLOSING SARA'S bedroom door behind him was one of the hardest things Nat had done in a long time. He wanted to lie down beside her and hold her. Wanted to feel that wild, red hair spreading over his chest. Wanted to kiss away at least some of the hurt she carried inside her.

He had a strong suspicion it was what she wanted, too. But he couldn't do it. He wasn't afraid of facing a killer, but he was scared to death of any kind of emotional involvement. The wounds were still just too damn raw.

But he was involved. He wanted to protect Sara

and Kendra, but heaven help him, he wanted to make love with Sara, too. Desire ran hot inside him as he headed to the bathroom for a cold shower and hopefully a clear-thinking mind.

THE HIGH SCHOOL was the same in name and location, but everything else was different. The old building had been razed seven years earlier and replaced with a new, modern structure with lots of narrow windows and a red brick exterior.

It was after ten when they got there, and the students were in class. They went right to the main office, where a couple of women worked behind a long counter that served to separate visitors from what looked like a row of small offices to the rear.

Nat took over, which was fine with Sara. He told the clerk who they were and that they would like to examine Sara's records while at the school.

"I can give you a printout of your transcript," she said, addressing her response to Sara. "If you want more than that, you'll have to talk to the principal first."

"The transcript will do for starters," Nat said.

"It will take me about ten minutes to pull it all together," she said. "You can wait here or you can wait in the conference room. No one's using it this morning."

"We'll wait here."

The ten minutes stretched to twenty. Sara spent the time trying to remember what high school had been like. Basically she remembered being a loner. She hadn't dated at all. Actually she'd never dated all that much, not even after leaving Meyers Bickham.

Steven had been her first serious relationship. As

it turned out, it hadn't been all that serious for him, not even after he'd signed the marriage license. He'd had affairs almost from day one, though she hadn't learned of them until later.

"Here's your transcript, Mrs. Murdoch. I just need you to sign for it."

Sara signed the release form, then picked up the printed transcript of her grades. Nat read over her shoulder.

"Pretty impressive. Straight A's," Nat said."

"Except for this C in Physical Education and another in Home Economics."

"Well, there goes your chance of getting a scholarship in playing ball or boiling water."

"I'd have probably learned to boil water if I'd stayed longer. The grades only go through the first half of my sophomore year."

"That's as long as you were here," the clerk said. "You moved."

"Is that what her records indicate?" Nat asked.

"Yes. That's what this asterisk with the number one after it means. See, it explains it on the bottom."

Sara scrutinized the small print. Asterisk—Moved to a new school. "Can you find out which school I moved to?"

"No, because no one requested your records."

"Are you certain?" Nat asked, folding the transcript and putting it inside his shirt pocket.

"Yes. If your records had been forwarded, I would have seen a note of it while I was getting the transcript."

"Wouldn't that throw up some kind of red flag to the school?"

"No. Most of the time records are requested, but

not always. Sometimes kids leave the country or go a private school that uses tests for placement instead of previous grades. And occasionally a student goes into homeschooling. I can probably get you in to see the principal now if you'd like to request that your entire folder be copied. I don't think it's a problem. It's just that no one has asked for more than transcripts since I came to work here."

Nat shuffled his feet, obviously eager to be on his way. "What kind of additional information would that give us?"

"Attendance records. Any correspondence about absenteeism. Health records. Just basic school record-keeping."

"I think this will do for now."

Sara thanked the woman for her time and followed Nat to his truck. "Nothing new. This matches what I told you."

"But it doesn't match your records at Meyers Bickham. And if your records are a lie, then there's no reason to think any of the other Meyers Bickham records are accurate."

"Which means that the records for the unidentified babies buried in the wall could have been faked," Sara said, trying hard to keep up with his pace as they walked to her van.

"Exactly. For all we know the orphanage just kept reporting them as residents after they were dead."

"And now they're willing to go to any lengths to keep that secret," Sara said. "Even after all these years."

"There's no statute of limitations on murder."

"Surely you don't think those babies were murdered?"

"I hope not."

So did Sara. Murdering babies would be so horribly depraved. Like attaching a skull to a doll's head. Or a ghostly parade in a dark, musty basement. Sara grabbed the passenger door as the world seemed to stop on its axis and start spinning backward.

"What's wrong?"

"I just remembered something new about that parade."

Chapter Ten

Nat opened the truck door for Sara and helped her inside. She looked a little shaky, and if she was going to fall apart on him, he didn't want it to be on the street in front of the high school.

"What is it you remembered?"

"I haven't thought of this in a long time. It's not in my nightmares anymore, but once, one of the people in the parade was carrying a large wicker laundry hamper."

Nat didn't see why thinking of that would upset Sara, but then she'd had a pretty traumatic week with no sign of things improving. "So what's with the hamper?"

"I'm not sure, but I now remember thinking it was strange that they were marching in file to do the laundry, or that ghosts would even have laundry."

Ghosts and a laundry basket. "Are we still talking about a nightmare?"

"Oh, Nat, I don't know. When it popped into my mind just now, it seemed so real, as if I were in that basement watching the strange procession pass."

"Real enough that you could see what was in the basket?"

"A blue blanket was sticking out the top, the kind they used in the nursery. I didn't know I even remembered that, but I do. There were blue blankets in boys' cribs and pink ones in the girls' cribs."

"You're talking real stuff now? Not nightmares but the orphanage nursery?"

"Yeah."

Sonofabitch. He didn't want to push her, but he had an idea she was on the verge of remembering something she'd spent years trying to forget. "Did you see inside the basket?"

"No, but what if you were right last night, and the parade in my nightmare stems from a real event? I may have witnessed a burial procession."

"That would explain the threats. Can you identify anyone from the procession?"

She shook her head, frustration lining her face. "I started to have the nightmares right after I was placed in the orphanage. That was twenty years ago. I was only ten."

"My guess is that you really saw that procession in the basement and the marchers weren't ghosts."

Sara leaned her head against the headrest and closed her eyes tight, massaging her temples as she did. Nat ran his arm along the back of the seat and let his hands tangle in her untamable red mane, wishing desperately there was some way to deal with this without hurling her headfirst into her troubled past.

"Everything is gray in my mind, Nat. It was dark and the person in front was carrying a gas lantern, the kind we used when we lost power at the orphanage due to a storm. But something must have made me think there was a baby in that hamper. Why else would I have been haunted all these years by the sound of a baby's cries?''

He had no idea, and his all-too-pragmatic mind was having trouble buying into the paranormal bent.

''I was sure the place was haunted right up until the day I ran away from there,'' Sara said.

''And now?''

''I don't know. Maybe it's haunted with the souls of the babies. Maybe I did see something and the babies are crying out to me for justice. I wonder if Sheriff Wesley can handle this,'' she said.

''I don't think we should tell him anything about the hamper or your nightmares.''

''But it could be important to the investigation.''

''Not unless you can identify the people you saw in the procession. We'll tell him about the cabin and the skull-topped doll, and about the mistake in your school records. That's all we know for certain.''

''You still think like an FBI agent.''

''Guess it gets in the blood.'' He laid his hand on her shoulder. ''But let's keep that quiet, too. I'm just Nat Sanderson, apple grower from North Georgia.''

''Whatever you say, apple grower.''

''So are you ready to pay a visit to the sheriff?''

''No, but I won't be any more ready if we put it off.''

He started the car while she punched in numbers on her cell phone. He didn't have to ask who she was calling. He knew it was Dorinda, to check on Kendra. Her past might be a one-eyed monster out to tear her into shreds, but her concerns were all for her daughter.

And after that she'd call the hospital to check on

Raye Ann, who was still unconscious and listed as critical as of a couple of hours ago.

Sara was a hell of a woman. She deserved a hell of a man—one who still had a heart that was fully intact—which ruled him out.

A fact which he'd best sear into his brain, because every time he touched her, his body seemed to have other ideas.

THIS TIME THEY met with Sheriff Wesley in a café in downtown Trenton not far from the high school they'd just left. It took a minute to locate him in the midst of the early lunch crowd, but Nat finally spotted him at a table in the far back corner. Isolated enough that they could have a halfway private conversation, Nat decided, as he pulled out a chair for Sara.

"Good to see you again," the sheriff said, his words spilling out around a mouthful of food.

"It would have been nicer if we could have talked in your office," Nat said, extending his hand.

The sheriff wiped the grease from the fried chicken he was eating on a napkin and stood, shaking Nat's hand and giving Sara a two-finger wave and a nod. "Caught me at a bad time. It was either talk while I eat or have to make it another day. I got a meeting this afternoon with the state attorney general."

"Does the meeting have something to do with the Meyers Bickham case?" Sara asked.

"Doesn't everything these days? So did you come over here to tell me about that cabin you were living in burning to the ground?"

"So you already know about that?" Nat said,

watching as Wesley went back to gnawing on a chicken leg.

"Georgia ain't so big that word don't get around."

Nat propped his elbows on the table and leaned in a little closer. "Is that what the attorney general wants to see you about?"

"I doubt it. He's just trying to get a little publicity out of this Meyers Bickham situation while the media's harping on it every night. I sure as hell don't need his interferin' with my case. And who's to say the cabin's burning down wasn't an accident. Dahlonega is over a hundred miles from the old orphanage."

"Me, for one," Nat said.

"And what makes you an expert on the subject?"

Nat watched the sheriff's expression as he explained about the doll they'd found on the footbridge. Wesley stared at him, his eyes narrowed so much they almost closed.

"Guess the tape over the mouth means someone's still scared you know something and might talk," he said, addressing his words to Sara. "Do you?"

"No."

"Did you talk about this with reporters?"

"No."

"Good. The more this stuff leaks to the media, the bigger it will be blown out of proportion."

A waitress came to take their order. Both Nat and Sara ordered black coffee only. The sheriff had apparently finished eating since there was nothing more than a smidgen of white milk gravy left on his plate. He picked up his glass and downed half of the iced tea before he set it back on the table.

"There's more," Sara said, when the waitress

walked away. "We paid a visit this morning to the high school I attended when I lived at the orphanage."

"Reliving old times?"

"No. Checking records." She explained what they'd found, and suggested that the other records kept by Meyers Bickham couldn't be trusted.

"I don't know what you two think you're doing," Wesley said, "but you're messing around in a criminal investigation. If you have any leads or information you want to share about the case, I'd appreciate hearing them, but other than that it's plain dangerous for you to be getting involved with this."

"I don't see how visiting my old high school can be dangerous," Sara said.

"Just let the law handle this. That's all I'm asking."

The waitress returned with the coffee, but it was clear the sheriff was through talking. He yanked some bills from a money clip and plopped them down on the table.

"I gotta go folks. You need to do the same. Go back to the apple orchard and tend to the fruit. I'll take care of the MB investigation. And since you claim you don't know nothing, Mrs. Murdoch, just lay low for a couple of weeks. By then the whole thing will be a closed case."

"I wish I believed him," Sara said, as the sheriff hitched up his pants and strode toward the door.

"Guess we can hope for the best."

"Does that mean you're ready to trust all of this to him?"

"Sure. Right after I win the Boston Marathon." Nat slapped his bum leg for emphasis. "Drink up," he said, lifting his coffee cup in a mock toast. "And let's get of here and find some food that won't clog our arteries before we pay the bill."

TROY WESLEY gunned his engine and backed out of the parking lot. As if he didn't have enough problems he had to deal with Nat Sanderson. Apple grower from the Dahlonega area. Bull! Troy knew exactly who Nat was. Ex-FBI. Ex-high-priced bodyguard. A good sheriff always did his homework. But Troy didn't care what Nat had done in the past. He wasn't doing it now, and he didn't carry a dadgum bit of clout.

Still, Troy didn't need Nat's kind of trouble. He had more than enough coming at him from people who did have clout. All this over some dead orphans that didn't get a plot under a sycamore tree. Like they would know the difference. Like anyone had ever cared when they were alive.

NAT PULLED INTO a strip mall and stopped in front of a small deli while Sara made another call to check on Kendra. He killed the engine and waited until she was off the phone.

"Is this lunch?" she asked, her hand already on the door handle.

"I thought we might pick up something for a picnic. There are lots of scenic areas on our way home."

"I don't feel much like a picnic."

"You have to eat. It's either a noisy café or listening to the songs of birds under the trees."

"An easy choice when you put it that way."

Once inside, she seemed to get more into the spirit of the outing. She picked out potato salad, two kinds of olives from large pottery jars, a selection of cheeses and some crusty bread. Nat chose a bottle of Cabernet and a bunch of bright purple seedless grapes.

"Do you need plastic glasses and utensils?" the clerk asked as she bagged their purchases.

"That would be great. And we need the wine uncorked."

"Where are you folks from?"

"Over by Dahlonega."

"Then I don't have to tell you about the beauty of the Chattahoochee National Forest."

"I'm not familiar with this area," Nat admitted.

"Then you should take time to explore. We do a lot of camping around Keown Falls. It's absolutely gorgeous. Hidden Creek's nice, too."

"Thanks."

They took their bags and went back to the truck. A beautiful day. Great food. A beautiful woman.

And enough ghosts from both their pasts to make Halloween a year-round holiday.

NAT GAVE the driver's seat to Sara when they left the deli. Once they were on the highway, he borrowed her cell phone and called Bob Eggars. He was about hang up when Bob barked a breathless hello.

"Did I interrupt something?"

"An argument with Bilks."

"Why are you arguing with Bilks? I thought it was an established fact that he's an expert on everything."

"Well, now he's an expert on orphanages."

"Meyers Bickham?"

"How'd you guess?"

"Does that mean you have an official invite to the party?"

"Yep. Working with the local sheriff who, like our good buddy Bilks, is also an expert on everything. He's made it clear he doesn't want or need our interference."

"So who invited you to the show?"

"The Georgia attorney general, directly. Indirectly, it was the governor, or so I hear. The media's jumping all over the poor-dead-orphans angle."

"What grounds did they use to involve the Bureau?"

"Turns out the orphanage accepted a few out-of-state kids at one time, so that makes it fall under our jurisdiction."

"Did you draw the assignment?"

"Me and Johnny Bilks. This is my lucky day."

It wasn't really Bob's lucky day, but it could be Nat's. "Do you think you can get access to the adoption records for Meyers Bickham?"

"You're really getting into this."

"It's a fascinating mystery."

"Are you sure this isn't more than casual interest?"

"Can you get the records?"

"Actually I'll have copies of some of the most pertinent ones on my desk by five this afternoon."

"Are they still part of the public domain?"

"As far as I know. Will be until and unless some judge says they're not."

"Then I'd appreciate some information."

"In that case, give me the scoop, Mr. Peace-loving Apple Grower. What's this really about?"

Nat ignored the question. "I'd like to know how many babies were adopted from the orphanage."

"A total number?"

"Yeah, but I'd like a breakdown of when they were adopted. Names of adopting families would be nice if you have them."

"Most of those records are not public domain. Adopting families had the choice of keeping that information sealed."

"But you have it, right?"

"Not at the present time. But I'm one of those boring play-by-the-rules agents these days. I gave up all that Dirty Harry stuff."

"Marriage do that to you?"

"Marriage and a kid on the way."

"Congratulations."

"Thanks. Anything else you need to know about the now infamous MB?"

"Health records would be good."

"I don't think that will help any. The bodies weren't preserved in any way, so there's not enough left of them to do much more than DNA tests. I'm not sure there would have been much left of them anyway. Evidently the walls were cracked open in lots of places and the basement was overrun with large rats. Large, *hungry* rats."

More of the nightmare that bore a striking resemblance to reality. "Guess there's no dental records, either?"

"No. Too young for that."

"Still, I'd like to see what you have."

"I'll give you a call in the morning. You got a place I can fax them yet, or you still going courier?"

"Courier for now."

"Be careful down there, buddy. I do not think that sheriff likes people playing in his death pit. And he might be the least of your worries if you actually get onto something."

"Why? You know details you're not sharing with me?"

"Just that there's at least one high-stake player linked with the administration of MB. There were two, but Senator Marcus Hayden was murdered back in January."

"I didn't see his name or anyone else's I recognized on the list you sent me."

"That's because their names were somehow purged from the written records."

"Just one of those slips of the eraser?"

"Or the shredder."

"So who was there besides Marcus?"

"You didn't hear it from me, okay?"

"Of course not. You play by the rules."

Nat let out a low whistle as he wrote down the name of the newest MB heavyweight.

"So what did you learn?" Sara asked, when he broke the connection.

"Does the name Judge Cary Arnold mean anything to you?"

SARA SAT Indian style on a carpet of pine straw and sipped her wine, her mind struggling to make sense of things. It was all happening so fast, like sitting in the middle of a train track with the locomotive roaring toward you. From seemingly harmless threats to a burned down cabin and an attack on Raye Ann in Sara's apartment. From a vacation-for-two cabin to living with a man who jolted her senses with a touch.

But if the changes had been fast for her, they seemed to be even faster for Nat. He didn't look or act like the man she'd met the night she was search- ing for the cabin. No beard. No long, scraggly hair. No reluctance to get involved. It was as if he thrived on danger, got off on finding ways to outsmart a killer adversary.

Nat finished off the potato salad and walked over and sat down beside her. "Have you remembered anything about the judge?"

"The name doesn't seem familiar. I don't remem- ber much about the administration. I saw a lot of one female doctor that first year when I was having the nightmares and waking up screaming every night."

"Do you remember her name?"

"No, but I'd probably remember her face. At least, I would if I could see a photo from twenty years ago. And I'd probably remember her name if I heard it. She was a lifesaver. The only person who seemed to understand what I was going through."

"So you told her about the nightmares?"

"Sure."

"And the procession marching through the base- ment?"

"I'm sure I did. She's the one who helped me get past the horrors."

"How did she do that?"

"Oh, Nat, you're asking me about things from twenty years ago when I was still dealing with losing my mother. I think she gave me some meds to help me sleep. Mostly I just remember her talking to me, telling me that the nightmares were part of the trauma and that I should try not to think about them.

Which is exactly what I've tried to do for twenty years.''

She finished the wine and set her glass on the ground beside her. "It's hard to believe I ever went down into that basement when I was so terrified of the nightmares. And if I didn't go down there, then I couldn't have seen that procession."

"The rats were real. I heard that from Bob Eggars today." He didn't want to say more, didn't want to go into the gory details of how they'd fed on the bodies, but he could tell from Sara's pasty coloring and drawn expression that she'd put two and two together.

"Dark and musty and full of rats." Her voice trailed to a scratchy whisper.

"We could drive up to the site of the orphanage this afternoon and see if that triggers some memories. It's not far."

Her lungs constricted, and she felt as if something had sucked the oxygen from them. "I can't go there, Nat."

"There's nothing there that can hurt you now. Whether the images that haunt you were real or really are just nightmares, they're not going to come to life and drag you back into the basement."

"You're a lot surer of that than I am."

"The basement doesn't exist anymore except as a hole in the ground."

"I'm sorry, Nat. But I just can't go there. Not yet. I can't deal with all of that on the top of present danger."

"Then we should probably get started back." He stood, took her hands and pulled her to a standing position.

Only he didn't let go. So they stood there, toe to toe, in the shade of the pine trees with the tickle of a summer breeze on their skin, and desire that shouldn't exist at a time like this creating a shimmering heat between them.

It made no sense. Life made no sense. She hadn't had any kind of feelings for a man since Steven had left eighteen months ago, so why now, when she was dealing with one terror after another?

Finally he let go of her hands, but instead of moving away, he rested them on her shoulders and let his thumbs trail her collarbone.

She knew he was going to kiss her. It was what she wanted, but still she pulled away, plagued by the old insecurities.

"Were you ever married, Nat?"

"Yes. Long enough to celebrate our six-month anniversary."

"What happened?"

"My bride decided marriage wasn't for her, so she just moved out of the apartment one day while I was at work."

"Do you still love her?"

"I'm not sure I ever loved her, but we were great in bed together and at twenty-two I thought that was what it was all about."

"But you have been in love."

"That didn't sound much like a question."

"It wasn't. I'm no relationship guru, but I'm smart enough to know that when a man goes into the kind of hibernation you did, there's bound to be a woman behind it."

"There was a woman."

"Tell me about her."

He walked away, propped his hand against the trunk of a towering pine tree and stared at the craggy drop-off. "This has nothing to do with us, Sara."

"It does if there's ever going to be an us."

He turned back to her, his eyes showing the now-familiar black depths that frightened her with their intensity.

"Her name was Maria Hernandez."

Chapter Eleven

Nat let the old memories crawl back into his mind, unsure which emotions they'd evoke. Sometimes guilt was the strongest. Sometimes anger. Sometimes it was just the image of the small limp body and the blood that seemed to gush like a hot spring. And always there was the ache, so strong it seemed to encompass every cell of his body.

"My job was to protect the family of a South American government official who was in Washington seeking financial aid for his country. Supposedly he was trying to break the hold that drug dealers had on the throats of his people, and he was afraid that members of the cartel would strike at him through his wife and daughter. Maria was his wife."

"What was she like?"

Nat fell back in time, to the first time he'd seen Maria. "She was exotic, dark skin, so soft and smooth it seemed to almost melt if you touched it. She had long black hair that fell straight to the middle of her back and dark, expressive eyes. When she looked at me and smiled, I thought I'd been transported to another world."

Nat turned and walked back to the edge of the

cliff. The precipitous drop-off seemed appropriate for the way he felt right now. "Meeting Maria was the beginning of the end."

"Because she was married?"

"No, because she was as venomous and virulent as any snake that ever slithered into a man's path. And because I was fool enough to be taken in by her." He propped his hand against a nearby tree, leaning against it for support.

This was the first time he'd said any of this out loud though he'd gone over it a million times in his mind. Talking about it was painful, but not as bad as he'd expected. Evidently time and distance did have some healing powers. Or maybe it was just that Sara was so easy to talk to.

"Bottom line was I fell in love with her, at least with the person I thought she was. And I was crazy about her daughter. Liana was the perfect mix of her parents. She had her mother's beauty and her father's way of facing the world head-on, like a bull with no fear of the bullfighter."

"How old was she?"

"Four."

"The same age as Kendra." Sara put her hand over her mouth as if she could stop the words and the thoughts that must be filling her mind. "Is that why you helped us that first night, Nat, because Kendra reminded you of Liana?"

"Not consciously, but it probably entered into it."

"And then you got stuck with us."

"No." Finally he turned and faced Sara. "My inviting you to the house wasn't due to what happened before. It was in spite of it."

She sighed and stared at the ground long seconds

before meeting his gaze again. "Where's Maria now?"

"In prison. For conspiring to have her husband murdered."

Sara hugged her arms around her chest, as if she'd been hit by a frigid blast of cold air. "Did you..." She exhaled sharply, as if steeling her nerves. "Did you kill him?"

"I didn't fire the bullet, but I didn't stop it, either. And I didn't stop the ricocheted bullet that killed Liana." His voice faltered as the pain exploded inside him. It was almost as if the bullets were firing again. Only this time they were erupting in his chest and tearing away the muscle and tissue of his heart.

"Oh, Nat. Only four years old. How horribly sad."

"No one meant to kill her, but she was dead all the same. I didn't even see it coming. But I should have, and I would have if I hadn't been convinced that Maria was telling me the truth and that the guys who did the shooting were there to keep her husband from killing her. I was caught off guard, the cardinal sin of any man sworn to protect."

Sara stood and stepped closer. "What a pair we are, Nat Sanderson. Both of us so screwed up by our past that we're stuck in a time warp. You with heartbreak, guilt and regret. Me with buried memories and nightmares that seem to be taking on new life."

"There's one big difference. None of your problems were of your doing."

"You made an all-too-human mistake, Nat. You trusted the wrong person. But withdrawing from life won't change anything."

"I never expected it to make things right. I'm just trying to find a way to live with myself."

"By saving me and Kendra. Don't get me wrong, Nat, I'm not complaining. I don't know what I'd be doing right now without you, but you're not the monster you see yourself as. Not in my book, anyway." She put out her hand and he took it. Her skin wasn't soft the way Maria's had been. She didn't melt at his touch.

Sara was real and strong and honest. At least he saw her that way. But then his judgment had been dead wrong before.

"Let's get out of here, Nat. I want to go pick up Kendra now and hold her close for as long as she'll let me."

Nat understood the feeling. It was exactly what he wanted to do with Sara, but he knew she needed time to digest all he'd told her. He helped her gather the remains from their impromptu picnic. Strange. The attraction between them was still as strong as ever, but sharing his darkest secrets with her had added a new layer of complexity to the relationship.

He didn't understand the new feelings anymore than he understood the initial ones. All he knew was that he wanted to be with her. And that he wanted to kiss her again—and more.

"MOMMY, MOMMY, guess what?"

Sara grabbed her daughter, held her close until Kendra squirmed loose from her grasp. "Let me see." Sara rested her chin on her finger as if in deep thought. "You rode elephants through the jungle."

"No, silly, Mommy. I helped Mr. Henry pick cu-

cumbers and squash and he took me for a ride on his tractor. We were sooooo high.''

''Now that sounds like a fun day.''

''It was. Dorinda and I made Snickerdoodles!''

''I smell them,'' Nat said, sniffing the aroma of cinnamon and baking dough that wafted through the house. ''So do we get to sample some of those cookies?''

''You betcha, uh, Dorinda?'' Kendra said, leading the way to the kitchen.

''You betcha, girl. As long as they save plenty for the pastry chefs.''

''That's us,'' Kendra said, just in case they didn't know what a pastry chef was.

Sara relaxed for the first time that day. It wasn't that she didn't expect Kendra to be perfectly safe and well cared for at the Callahan's farm. She'd have never left Kendra if she hadn't been convinced of that.

But with the terrors coming in waves, there was no way for her not to worry if Kendra was out of her sight. And now she had the image of a young South American girl in her mind, shot to death at the same age Kendra was now.

They stayed for cookies and milk, and Henry loaded them up with fresh vegetables before they left.

''Mattie's not going to like you giving away the profits,'' Nat said.

''She won't mind. She just runs that store so she can yak all day and keep up with the neighbors. I could make more money selling it to the local grocers, but then I'd have to be the one listening to her all day.''

And as much as Sara was sure Henry adored his wife, she was also pretty sure he was telling the truth. She paid Dorinda for her baby-sitting services then thanked them both again as the three of them climbed into her van.

"Did you know that there's a gold mine in Dahlonega?" Kendra said. "A real one."

"I've heard that," Nat said. "What do you say we go and pan for gold?"

"Yeah. Let's do it, Mr. Nat. Let's go get us some gold."

"Gold?" Sara said, looking hard at Nat.

"The mine's been closed for years. Costs more to mine the metal than it's worth on today's market, but some of the richest veins in the eastern part of the States were right here in the Dahlonega area."

"So you're taking my daughter to a deserted mine? I don't think so."

"It's a tourist attraction. The new owner opened up a small part of the old mine for tours and he has an area where visitors can try their hand at panning for gold the way the old-timers did it. Well the way they would have liked to do it."

An old mine. Panning for gold. It was the type of local attraction she'd hoped to visit with Kendra this summer, before all their plans had gone up in smoke. But now, with the threats. "I'm not sure it's a good idea, Nat."

"It'll be fine, Sara. I wouldn't suggest it if I wasn't sure. And it is your and Kendra's vacation."

"Yeah, Mommy. It's our vacation."

"Whoppee," Sara said, with a total lack of enthusiasm. But it would definitely be a summer she wouldn't forget. If she lived to remember it.

CARY ARNOLD walked through the spacious living room of his plantation-style house, stopping to chat with one guest after another. The party was to raise money for an after-school program for Atlanta's poorer latchkey children, but it was like all the other galas his beautiful wife hosted for one charity or another.

Felecia gave new meaning to the old term trophy wife. Not only was she twenty years younger than him and so striking that no straight man ever passed without giving her a second look, she was smart and schooled in the ways of Atlanta's socially elite.

Old money. It offered a rank that couldn't be bought. You either had to be born into it or marry into it. Luckily Cary had married into it since he'd come from so far on the other side of the tracks, he'd had to hop on his bike to even reach the slums.

He'd done more than his share of underhanded deeds to reach the point where he was today, but he'd do it all again without a second thought. He'd just cover his tracks better—especially with the Meyers Bickham fiasco. But he'd been much younger then, and he'd have screwed over a crippled veteran if that's what it had taken to climb Georgia's social and economic ladder. As it was, Meyers Bickham was one of the lesser sins he'd committed. It was just getting the most attention.

Which is why he'd made sure Abigail and her husband were on the guest list tonight. He scanned the room, and when he didn't see her, he grabbed a bacon-wrapped shrimp from the tray of a passing waiter, slid it between his lips and walked to the bar that had been set up on the veranda.

And there was Abigail, looking pretty in pink. Her

brown hair was piled on top of her head with loose tendrils curling about her cheeks. She was close to his age, nearing fifty, but she still had a firm, shapely body and very few wrinkles, no doubt the result of the best plastic surgery money could buy.

He got a Scotch on the rocks and waited until she'd finished her conversation with one of the state senators before he walked over. "Glad you could make it tonight, Abigail."

"I try never to miss any of Felecia's events."

"Let's take a walk to the garden."

"Tell me it's to see some new kind of rose your gardener has found and not to talk business."

"You know what it's about."

She frowned. "In that case, I need my drink freshened." She handed Cary her glass. "A vodka martini."

"I know. Extra dry with two olives."

"Nice to have a man remember."

He went for the drink, then found her waiting on the garden path. Fortunately no one else had ventured this far from the food and the booze yet.

"I can't believe that lunatic attacked some professor staying in Sara's apartment," he whispered, once he was certain they were out or earshot of the other partygoers.

"According to the cops, Raye Ann Jackson was injured in a fouled burglary attempt."

"And you know that's not true. The guy was always a hothead."

"I don't remember him quite that way."

"Well, I didn't sleep with him, so naturally my opinion would be slanted a little different than yours."

"Have you talked to him?" she asked.

"As a matter of fact I have."

"And what did he tell you?"

"To leave everything to him."

"That sounds like an excellent idea to me," Abigail said. "And I can assure you he didn't attack anyone in Columbus. Actually, I thought that blunder sounded more your speed, Cary."

"I'm not a blundering idiot. I'm a federal judge and I plan to stay one."

"Good for you."

"We need to make certain Sara doesn't squeal."

"When will you get it into your head that she has no idea what went on in that basement?"

"How can you say that, as many times as you talked to her about what she saw?"

"That's why I can say it. It was all just a frightening nightmare to her. I made sure of that."

"But suppose she figures it out?"

"When did you become such a disgusting sniveler, Cary? I remember when you were a tough scrapper and not afraid of anything."

"That was before I had anything to lose."

"Who do you think is going to figure this all out? It's not like the FBI is in on the investigation. It's small-town stuff being handled by a small-time county sheriff. The orphanage doesn't even exist any longer. There is nothing to worry about."

"The scandal has been on the news every night this week."

"Only because it's summer and there's nothing else going on. Give it a few days. Some politician will grope somebody or some famous ball player will punch a guy out in a bar somewhere. Then the focus will shift and our little babies in the brick graves will be forgotten.''

"You always make things sound so simple, Abigail. That's how we got into all of this in the first place. You made it sound so simple."

"It still is, Cary." She put her hand on his arm. "So just go back to your party and your beautiful wife and forget that Meyers Bickham ever existed." She took a mirror from her small black handbag and checked her hair.

"It's perfect, as always," Cary said, but remembering times when he'd seen it mussed, had seen her naked. Memories that still got him all hot and bothered if he let them hang around too long.

"Thanks," Abigail said, returning the mirror to her handbag. "Now let's go back before someone misses us and wonders where the two of us have gotten off to."

He watched as she turned and walked away. So damn self-assured. Some things never changed.

He turned and stared at his house, lights glowing, the sounds of laughter spilling from the open doors and the veranda and carrying all the way to the garden. It was clear he couldn't count on Abigail's help, but he was not going down. No matter what it took, he was not going down.

SARA STOOD on the back porch and watched the black clouds rolling in as the wind whipped her hair into her mouth and eyes and sent her white cotton nightgown flying high enough to have shown her panties if anyone had been around to see.

But she was alone. Kendra was tucked in bed and sleeping soundly, though she probably wouldn't be for long if the thunder that rolled in the distance kept getting closer.

Nat had disappeared into his own room just after he'd helped with the dinner dishes, but she'd heard the water blasting through the old pipes while she'd read Kendra a bedtime story, so she knew he'd come out long enough to shower.

He'd been unusually quiet since they'd returned to this house. Neither of them had mentioned the day's confession of his love for Maria, yet she was certain it was on his mind the same way it was on hers.

He'd fallen in love with an exotic beauty who'd used him and led him into a deadly mistake. He talked as if he hated Maria now, and maybe he did, but Sara wasn't convinced of that. She'd heard it said before that the line between hate and love could be as thin as a cat's eyelash.

She couldn't help but compare herself to the woman with silky black hair and skin so soft it seemed to melt when he touched it. He'd called Maria beautiful.

No one in all her life had ever called her beautiful. Not even Steven. He'd said she was dependable, spunky, intelligent—even that her eyes were fiery and that she turned him on—but never had he said she was beautiful.

If he had she would have known he was lying. She had eyes and mirrors. Her legs were too long and a tad too skinny. Her hair was too red. Her breasts were too small. At best she was plain, and at best meant when she had on her makeup and had taken the time to do something more than pull her wild hair back from her face and try to contain it—which wasn't all that often.

A jagged bolt of lightning lit the sky, followed by a clap of thunder that rattled the windows behind her. She listened to see if Kendra awoke, but there was no noise except that of the wind rattling the wooden door of the shed and rustling the leaves as it swept through the tree branches.

The screen door behind her squeaked. She turned just as Nat joined her on the porch, barefoot, dressed only in jeans.

"Looks like a bad one," Nat said, walking over to stand beside her. "Not good for apples."

She grabbed the skirt of her nightgown and held it in place as best she could. "Will you lose many to the wind?"

"I could, if it gets worse." He leaned over the railing so that he could see to the corners of the house. "Have you seen Mackie?"

"Not lately. Actually not since I brought Kendra inside for dinner, but you said he usually sleeps in the shed."

The lightning struck again, frighteningly close and in a vertical pattern that made it appear as if it were aiming at a target in the backyard. The thunder that followed was practically eardrum-shattering.

"I better check on Kendra." She went inside and stood at the door to her daughter's bedroom. Still sound asleep. Evidently a day on the farm had worn her out.

Sara tiptoed away to the sound of rain pelting against the windows. She went to the back door to close it, but Nat was still out there, standing on the porch and staring into the storm though the wind was driving the rain onto the porch. Raindrops dripped off the hairs on his chest and soaked the front of his jeans.

"It's not like Mackie to stay out in a storm," he said. "He's afraid of thunder. Runs to the porch and barks to be let in at the first loud clap. I'm going to look for him."

"You'll get caught in the storm."

"I won't go far, but I want to check around the yard. Just in case."

Just in case. Sara felt as if someone had turned a key inside her, opened a door that loosed a kind of nebulous dread that infiltrated her whole body at once. She held on to the door for support, her legs rubbery and her brain growing numb.

The terrors were nonstop, but surely they hadn't reached out to include Mackie. Only why wouldn't they? The notes, the fire, Raye Ann—none of it made sense except in some crazed psycho's mind, so why should this?

Nat whistled one more time and then started down the back steps and into the driving rain. She ran after him, to stop him. "Wait, Nat!"

"Get back inside, Sara. There's no use for both of us to get drenched."

A streak of lightning illuminated the night. She spotted the small pistol all but hidden in the palm of Nat's hand at the same time they heard Mackie's wail. He was at the edge of the back lawn, near the path that led down to the orchard, limping toward the house.

Nat took off running with Sara right behind him. Only Nat was slowed by his own limp and Sara reached Mackie first. His right forepaw was slit open and bleeding. "Oh, you poor thing. You look as if you tangled with a wildcat."

The next loud clap of thunder hit, and Mackie propelled himself into her arms, hurt foot and all.

He would have been heavy dry and he seemed to weigh a ton wet, but she took off running with him. When they reached Nat, he relieved her of the load and she raced up the stairs and held the door open as Nat carried Mackie in and put him down on the kitchen floor.

Mackie shook off the water, sharing the wet wealth with the whole kitchen as Sara ran for a supply of older bath towels. When she got back, Nat was examining the paw.

"How bad is it?"

"Not as bad as it looked at first. It's not a clean cut, though. Looks like he probably got it caught in something and yanked it loose, tearing the flesh in the process."

"What would he get it caught in?"

"Don't go reading anything into this, Sara. He's a country dog with acres to roam in. He did more damage than this one day chasing a squirrel in the shed and getting his paw stuck in the slats of an apple crate."

"I think you should call the vet."

"Not at ten o'clock at night. I'll douse the tear with peroxide, coat it with an antibiotic cream and bandage it. Then if it looks bad in the morning, we'll see the vet."

Nat stood and left the task of towel drying Mackie to her while he went after the first-aid supplies. Mackie licked her hands and face while she dried him, perking up now that he was inside the dry kitchen with his adoring fans to pamper him and tend his wound.

"You pour, I'll hold," Nat said, handing her a bottle of peroxide. He picked up Mackie and held his wounded paw over the kitchen sink. To her surprise, Mackie only whimpered as the peroxide foamed on the cut.

Once that was done, Mackie sprawled on the floor, his tail thumping against the old linoleum as Nat bandaged the paw. "I'll get that for you, she said, reaching over the dog to cut the strip of adhesive tape.

She was aware of Nat's stare as she reached for it. His hands were still on Mackie, but his gaze had fastened on her. Soaking wet. Her gown sticking to her as if it were glued in place. Her breasts outlined against the fabric of her gown.

His fingers slipped and the bandage he'd wound in place started to unravel. The room grew incredibly warm as if all the moisture had turned to steam. But the real heat was inside her, desire running so hot she could barely breathe.

"I've got to go," she said. "Take a shower." She didn't even know if she was making sense, but she had to get out of the room quick or she'd be in Nat's arms, and feeling the way she did right now, she didn't think it would end with just a kiss.

She backed out of the room, aware that Nat was still staring at her while Mackie unwound the rest of the bandage.

NAT FINALLY MANAGED to get the bandage taped in place. The rain was still pelting against the windows, but all Nat heard was the water rattling the old pipes as it rushed to the shower. A few feet away, Sara was standing under the warm spray. Sexy, sweet, indescribable Sara.

His body was rock-hard, desire like he thought he'd never feel again pummeling his system and making mush of his mind. A man should never get emotionally involved with the woman he was protecting, but there was no denying that he was involved.

He should lock himself in his bedroom right now. But he walked in the other direction, toward the bathroom. He started to knock then changed his mind, turned the knob and opened the door.

The room was steamy, but then so was he. "Do you have room for two in there?"

"I thought you'd never ask."

Chapter Twelve

Nat's arousal made it damn near impossible to peel off the wet jeans. But he managed, then reached back to lock the bathroom door, just in case Kendra woke and came padding down the hall looking for her mother.

He pushed back the curtain and stepped into the large, claw-footed tub with Sara, into the steam and the heat. The way he was feeling, he would have expected to pounce on her like a high school kid at his first necking session. But he didn't move. He just stood there breathing hard, suddenly scared to death. It had been three and a half years since he'd been with a woman. Suppose he couldn't function at all?

But Sara stepped inside his arms and the fears vanished into the sultry vapor that enveloped them. Her body was soapy and slick, and he shuddered at the feel of her breasts against his chest and her thighs sliding against his.

She lifted her mouth to his, her pink lips wet and shimmery. When his mouth touched hers, the blood seemed to rush from his head, leaving him so dizzy he almost fell backward. Woozy and drunk on a million emotions that would bury him if he stopped to think about them.

But he wasn't thinking. He was just reacting, his body alive and fueled by a savage hunger that didn't seem to belong to the man he'd become. It was the old Nat. The one who dove into life with no holds barred.

He kissed her over and over, all the while letting his hands roam her back, down to her waist and over the curve of her soapy buttocks. He lifted her just a little, so that he could feel her slippery body slide over his member.

Desire shot through him so hard he thought he might explode without even entering her, but somehow he held back. He wanted to see her, to touch all of her, to run his tongue over her nipples and dip his fingers into her secret places. He wanted her to moan with pleasure, fight the mounting pressure until she was so ready for him that her insides were as hot and slick as her flesh.

"Let me look at you, Sara." He stepped back enough that his gaze could move from the tip of her head to her painted toenails.

"I'm not much to see," she whispered.

"You look great to me." Better than great. She was so real, so natural—so Sara, but with the red hair at the apex of her thighs holding onto glistening droplets of water and tiny rivulets dripping from the tips of her nipples. He cupped her breasts. Perfect handfuls. Still cradling them in his hands, he kissed first one and then the other.

"Oh, Nat. How did we get to here?"

"Compliments of Mackie." He knew that wasn't what she meant but if he tried to talk in the shape he was in, he'd say the wrong thing and disappoint her. And disappointed was the last thing he wanted her to be tonight. He kissed and stroked her, then dipped his fingers inside her.

"Oh, Nat." She moaned his name, and dug her hands into his back. "If you keep doing that, I won't be able to wait for you."

"Don't wait."

"I want you inside me." She slid her hands between them until her fingers touched his erection. Stroking him gently, she guided him to her, then wrapped her arms around his neck, as he slid inside her.

"Oh, Sara. Sara," he whispered, reeling with a need so strong it consumed him.

Thoughts raced through his mind. Things that a man should say, but with desire and need ravaging his body, he'd never make them sound right.

How could he say that if he'd dared to dream, he still wouldn't have thought it could ever be like this, that she was…driving him over the edge.

The blood roared in his head and coursed in his veins with the power of a raging river. He thrust inside her, again and again until he exploded in a sky-high eruption that left him barely able to breathe.

He held her close, the thin stream of warm water still flowing between them, his heart still hammering. The two of them in an antique tub, naked and passion spent. The moment grew awkward as he dreaded that she might expect some vow of love or commitment. Some promise that he could probably never keep.

He should have known better. Sara rose on her tiptoes and kissed him again, this time light and teasing, her voice breathlessly seductive. "When you come to life, Nat Sanderson, you really come to life.''

"I had help.''

"It was probably the drenched rat look.'' She trailed her fingers down his abdomen, as if to see if she could affect him again, and it was starting to work.

"You wash my back, and I'll wash yours,'' she said, soaping a cloth and handing it to him.

"You've got a deal.''

But no matter how light she made the moment, they'd crossed a line when they'd made love. Gone from fragile friends to lovers.

He'd decide what to do about it later, but right now he just had to make certain that the emotions didn't interfere with the protecting. That was a mistake he could never make again.

SARA KICKED at the sheet, rolled over, punched her pillow a few times and tried yet again to find a comfortable position in the bed that had seemed perfectly comfortable until tonight. Nat was sleeping a few doors down, probably snoring away without a thought of her while she couldn't get him or the fact that they'd made love off her mind.

If they'd had only themselves to think about, she'd probably be in his bed now, curled up beside him, close enough to hear his breathing and to feel his body heat. But it wasn't just them. There was Kendra, and she'd had enough changes in her life without dealing with a strange new relationship between her mother and Mr. Nat.

And there was the Meyers Bickham situation. She'd almost forgotten it during the passion of making love, but that was the only time it had slipped her mind for even a second. The danger was always there, as omnipresent as the air they breathed.

She flopped over again, this time settling on her back and staring at the ceiling. Not that she could actually see it. The storm had blown over but the night was still pitch dark, the stars and moon shut out by a heavy layer of low-hanging clouds. The same way the clouds of Meyers Bickham were hanging over her life.

Finally Sara began to drift into the desultory state between sleep and wakefulness when the mind traveled through a seamless collage that mixed reality with the imaginary.

A baby was crying. A ghost baby. *Let's hold hands. Just hold hands and be very, very quiet.*

She tried to figure out whose hand she was holding, but her eyes had closed and the thoughts drifted away with the quiet and steady breathing of sleep.

MORNING BROUGHT sunshine and a huge FedEx package filled with copies of financial, operating, and personnel records from the now defunct orphanage. Nat had the records spread out on the kitchen table and he'd been making notes for the past half hour. Sara had been busy with Kendra, getting her fed and dressed and settled into the day.

And she'd called the hospital again. Raye Ann was still unconscious from swelling in the brain, but her vital signs were strengthening. She was still in the ICU, and all the doctors were saying was that they could not rule out permanent brain damage.

No one other than Sara appeared to be linking the break-in and attack with the threats or the fire, but that didn't alter her opinion. She didn't know how it was linked any more than she knew why the eight "basement babies" hadn't had their deaths recorded or received proper burials, but she was becoming more and more determined to find out the answers to all the questions.

She'd spent years trying to forget, and this was where it had gotten her, sitting up here in the mountains waiting for the next disaster to strike. She couldn't even pay a visit to Raye Ann for fear the act would bring some new catastrophe into the woman's life. Everywhere that Sara went, disaster was sure to follow.

Sara stuck her head into the living room again to check on Kendra and Mackie. The lab was sitting on his rug by the living room hearth, watching Kendra cook pretend food for her dolls and stuffed animals using the set of plastic dishes and cookware Mattie had brought over while they were still in the cabin.

The most positive note of the day was that the large animal vet who took care of Henry's horses had stopped in first thing this morning and had declared Mackie's injury minor and had assured them they were treating the wound appropriately. He left medicine to ward off infection and suggested they keep Mackie inside so that even if he tugged the bandage off, the wound would stay reasonably clean.

Sara joined Nat in the kitchen. He tapped the eraser end of his pencil against the tablet he'd been filling with notations as Sara poured herself a second cup of coffee. "I may have found something here."

"What's that?"

"Didn't you tell me that babies were usually adopted soon after they came to the orphanage?"

"Unless there was some reason they weren't adoptable. And even then, they usually went into foster homes. The orphanage was for the kids that no one wanted, like freckle-faced redheaded brats who woke up the whole place screaming about their nightmares."

"I would have adopted you."

"I think you have. So what have you found?"

"According to these records, the baby wing was almost always full."

"No way." Sara took the chair next to his and pulled it close enough that she could see what he was looking at.

"This reports anywhere from eighteen to twenty-four children under the age of two at the orphanage at all times," Nat said, highlighting the numbers.

"It was more like five to six."

"Are you sure?"

"Not about all the years, but I worked in the nursery every weekend for the last two years I was there. I'd say half a dozen babies would have been a lot."

"Creative record keeping," Nat said.

"The kind they used in reporting that I lived there until I was eighteen when I actually left three years before that."

"Seems they made a habit of reporting children in residence who were no longer there," Nat said.

"Maybe they were afraid the state would close the place if it didn't have a full house."

"That probably figured into it," Nat agreed. "And a full house also got them more money." Nat slid some computer printouts from a brown envelope and stacked them in front of him. "The program was funded according to head count. So if they were paid for children or infants who were no longer there, that was money that could line someone's pockets.''

"So basically they were stealing from orphans,'' Sara said. "A new twist on stealing candy from a baby. And it had to be someone high enough in the scheme of things that they could get by with it.''

"More likely a joint effort,'' Nat said. "On-site administrators with no qualms about faking the records and at least one government supervisor who either didn't bother to verify the records or else was willing to play along—for a price, of course. Dirty secrets that have stayed hidden for a long, long time, and probably would have stayed secret forever if the bodies hadn't been dug up.''

"I must be missing something,'' Sara said. "I don't see any connection between money and the poor babies who were buried in the wall.''

"Maybe they were the unadoptable that you talked about. Only they might have been the ones even foster parents wouldn't take for one reason or another. Poor health. Handicapped. Whatever.''

Sara winced, fighting a new round of dread but not ready to buy into it. "You still think those infants were murdered, don't you?''

"Murder's the only thing I know that would explain why someone's so desperate not to have their secrets uncovered at this late date.''

"Because there's no statute of limitations on murder?''

"That and the fact that the punishment can be death or life imprisonment.''

She shook her head. "I can believe there was illegal transfer of funds going on and some tampering with the records, but not murder.''

"How can you be so sure?" Nat said. "You hated the orphanage so much you went to live on the streets at fifteen. And you can't even stand to think about the place. You practically went into meltdown yesterday when I suggested we stop by there."

"I'm not denying I hated living there. The caretakers were authoritarian and we were punished constantly for even the tiniest infraction of the countless rules. To this day I hate rules. I was embarrassed by the ugly clothes they gave us to wear. And there was the ridiculous lights-out and silence rules. Even in high school we were supposed to turn comatose at 10:00 p.m. And I never got to watch anything I wanted on…"

Sara exhaled sharply. "I'm doing it again, aren't I? My voice is rising and my hands are shaking, and all I'm doing is talking about the place."

Nat placed a hand on her shoulder. It was the first time he'd touched her since they'd made love last night. She was certain he meant to calm her, but his touch and the feelings it ignited just seemed to make this whole situation more complex and impossible.

How could she have become so intrigued by any man when her life was in such a mess? Only she wasn't just intrigued. It was a hundred times worse than that.

She was falling in love with Nat. Falling helplessly in love with a man who at worst might still be in love with another woman and at best was just starting to work his way free from a traumatic past that had sent him literally running for the hills.

She took a deep breath, determined to focus on the task at hand. "I don't think the babies were murdered, Nat. I may be naive, but I just don't think it's possible that anyone at Meyers Bickham actually killed a baby.''

''What makes you so sure?''

''Because I'm a mother. You can't take care of a helpless, totally dependent baby day after day and feel nothing.''

''There have been lots of cases where mothers kill their own babies.''

''But that's one person going nuts, not a concerted effort by seemingly rational people—running an orphanage no less.''

Nat stretched to a standing position and stood behind her, massaging her taut shoulders with his strong hands. ''You're amazing, Sara Murdoch. After all you've been through, you still can't face the fact that there are truly evil people out there.''

''That's not true. I think the psycho who set the cabin on fire is evil. I think the man who attacked Raye Ann is evil. I just don't buy that a group of people running an orphanage decided to murder eight babies for the little bit of money that would bring in. That's too macabre—like something from one of those horror movies that come out every Halloween.''

''I need some coffee,'' Nat said, evidently not wanting to get into this with her. ''Can I get you a cup?''

''No, but you can warm this.''

She handed him her half-empty cup then picked up a form that Nat had bled all over with his red pen. Names of staff members during the years she was living at the orphanage. She scanned the names. Mostly women. Probably caretakers or social workers. There were always a lot of those around. She remembered so few of them. Again, probably because she chose to block them from her mind.

"Here's a name I recognize," she said, zeroing in on a name halfway down the page. "Mary Ellen Spence."

Nat sat a cup of hot coffee at her elbow. "What do you remember about her?"

"She had a voice that would shatter glass—and that was when she was in a good mood. Get her riled and the woman could screech like a rabid owl. She and I had gotten into it the night before I left the place for good."

"What did you fight about?"

"I don't remember. I haven't thought of that in years. It just popped into my mind when I saw the name."

"She sounds charming."

"Right. So let me file that back in mind bank thirteen." She continued to scan down the list. "And here's another one I remember. Abigail Hoyt."

"Another screecher?"

"No, she was my lifesaver, the doctor I told you about who helped me deal with the nightmares and the loss of my mother."

"Dr. Hoyt, age twenty-eight. Unmarried. An intern who worked with the hospital. Getting ready to do her residency in pediatrics. Hmmm. Wonder if she could be Dr. Abigail Harrington?"

"Who is she?"

"The head of pediatrics at one of the hospitals in Atlanta and married to one of the richest men in Atlanta."

"Why do you think she was involved in Meyers Bickham?"

"It was one of the names Bob gave me, but he didn't think she was a major player or that she'd have access to or a reason for changing in-house records."

"If Harrington and Hoyt are one and the same, I'm certain she wasn't part of the illegal burials."

"And possible murders."

She shook her head, then brushed the flyaway red mane back from her face. "You are really hung up on that murder bit, Nat, but you'll have to look somewhere else. *My* Doctor Hoyt would not have been involved in anything as demented as disposing of dead babies inside a basement wall."

They stayed at the table another hour, going over the records, looking for something to jump out at them. Nothing else did.

Kendra skipped into the room, dragging her stuffed bear in one hand and carrying a plastic teapot in the other. "Would you like some hot tea?" she asked. "'Cause we had a tea party and there's lots left."

Nat held out his cup. "I'd love some tea."

Kendra peeked inside the cup. "I can't put it in there. It would get mixed up with the coffee."

"What was I thinking?"

"My coffee's all gone," Sara said. "You can pour me some tea."

Kendra lifted the teapot and poured her pretend tea, then set her teapot on the edge of the table. She reached over and grabbed Nat's arm. "I'm tired of cooking. So are we going to go get our treasure or not?"

"That's right. I promised you we'd pan for gold today."

"I'm not sure we should leave Mackie that long," Sara said, giving him an out.

Nat picked up a stack of papers, hit them on the table to line them up, then started shoving them into a large brown envelope. "We won't be gone long. Mackie will probably enjoy the quiet so he can nap. And Blake's coming over this afternoon to do some organic spraying, so he can look in on Mackie."

"Then I guess we're off to pan for gold," Sara said.

"And lunch," Nat added. "Henry claims there's a greasy spoon in Dahlonega that serves the best hamburgers and fried apple pies in the whole state of Georgia. But first I have to make a phone call to Bob Eggars. I want to see exactly who would have handled the transfer of money between the state and the orphanage. And I'd like to tell him about the discrepancy between what you remember about the number of babies in residence and what the records say."

Nat's hand brushed hers as he reached for the papers on her end of the table. Just an incidental touch, yet her pulse quickened. There was too much between them now for it to be any other way. And it was not only the physical act of making love that had changed things. It was the mingling of minds and the shared pasts. They were just too deep into each others lives to ignore the sexual energy that sizzled between them.

She sighed and pushed back from the table. Hamburgers, fried pies, gold and the horrifying thought that someone might have murdered infants for a few measly dollars. All that and wondering what she'd do tonight if Nat wanted a repeat of last night's stellar performance. Worse, wondering if she'd survive if he didn't.

Kendra followed her down the hall when she went to the bedroom to get the sunscreen. "Isn't this fun, Mommy?"

"It's a blast."

SARA HAD TO give it to Nat. The trip into Dahlonega had been a great idea. A taste of normalcy in a world gone mad helped to put things in perspective. They were dealing with a lunatic but the rest of the world was going about life as usual. As soon as the person who was turning her life into a reality horror show was caught, her life would be normal again, too.

Well, normal except that she'd be back at her apartment in Columbus—without Nat. She couldn't stay in his house once the danger was past, and the cabin was probably no more than a pile of ashes. She didn't see him going back to the bearded recluse routine, but she didn't see him chasing after her in Columbus, either.

"Gold's not gonna just hop in your pan, Big Red."

She snapped out of the reverie when she realized the guide was talking to her. "So what do I do?"

"Do like Little Red." He turned his gaze to Kendra, who was holding her gold pan and stirring its contents with her index finger.

"Yep, there's gold in them thar hills," the man said. "'Course it's hot out in them thar hills, and there's mosquitoes and snakes out there, too."

Like the guy who'd given the tour of the mine, the two bearded men who were instructing them in the proper methods for panning were more than worth the price of admission. Their drawls were exaggerated, their coveralls baggy and their hats floppy, but they delivered their own brand of mountain humor as if it was totally impromptu, though Sara was certain they repeated pretty much the same routine all day long.

Nat wasn't panning. He was in full bodyguard mode, at least she guessed that was why he was standing back and watching everything. It gave her enough confidence that she plunged into the experience. And once she did, she got completely caught up in the process.

The art of panning was fairly easy once she got the hang of it, especially since they were doing it under the best of conditions—out of the sun and at waist-high troughs that eliminated the stooping an actual mountain stream would have required.

Sara watched as the guide demonstrated by taking a pan of sediment and submerging it beneath the water's surface. Then he tilted the pan away from him and quickly brought it out of the water, which washed away the lighter particles that had floated to the top while still leaving a good portion of the sediment in the bottom of the pan.

After that it was just a matter of slowly rotating and vibrating the pan, then pouring off the excess water and starting again. Doing one pan of sediment and watching the heavier metals sink to the bottom was interesting, Sara admitted. But the thought of doing it all day long, in all kinds of weather, stooped over a mountain stream, seemed too tedious for words. Which probably explained why panning for gold was pretty much a lost art.

Once the method was demonstrated, they were on

their own, except for Kendra and another youngster about her age who were getting lots of extra attention.

"I don't see my gold," Kendra protested, after they'd been at it a couple of minutes.

"Oh, it's in there," her helper said. "Probably enough to buy you a big wad of bubblegum so you can pop it and blow bubbles all the way home."

"My Mommy won't let me."

"Reckon you'll have to buy her a wad of gum, too. Better get one for your dad as well."

"Mr. Nat's not my dad. He's the apple man, but he used to have a beard like yours."

"You're kidding." The man looked over to Nat. "You had a nice mess of wiry hair like this and you shaved it off?"

"Afraid so."

"Well if I had me a good-looking redheaded woman like the one you've got there, I might even shave this one off."

"His old lady's a model," the other guy said.

That got everyone's attention.

"Yep. You've seen those dolls made of them old dried, wrinkled apples. His old lady was the model for them dolls. 'Course they had to airbrush her up a bit first."

"Look," Kendra squealed. "I do have gold."

"That there's fool's gold," one of the guides said. "Shiny but it don't spend."

But by the time they'd finished, Kendra had her gold, a speck of it floating in a tiny water-filled vial that she held onto as if it were worth a million dollars.

"What did you think?" Nat asked, as they walked to the car.

"It was a nice break, the kind of thing I thought Kendra and I would be doing when I planned the summer in the cabin. Local attractions. Waterfalls. Long hikes in the parks and the Chattahoochee Forest."

"The summer's not nearly over." He put a hand to the small of her back and his mouth close to her ear. "I heard from Bob while you were seeking your fortune. This will all be over soon, Sara."

Over soon. It sounded good. So why didn't she believe it?

WHATEVER NAT had heard he was apparently saving until they had a chance to talk without Kendra listening in on the conversation. But he found the restaurant Henry had recommended in under ten minutes.

Sara hadn't felt hungry at all when they'd parked in front of the rambling building but that had changed the second they opened the door and got a whiff of the odors. Cinnamon and nutmeg and frying apples meshed with onions and the piquant smell of barbecue sauce and roasting chickens.

"I like this place already," Nat said.

"The smells are mouthwatering," Sara said, grabbing Kendra's hand before she went exploring on her own or to join the family of six that she was already waving to.

"Yeah, but it's the paper towels, I like," he said. "A roll on every table."

"I didn't know you were so turned on by paper

towels. Maybe we should stop at the store on the way home and stock up.''

''Paper towels mean the burgers and barbecue will come dripping with sauce. If it's messy and dripping, it's got to be good, unless it's my bike and the runoff is oil.''

''No wonder women and men don't talk the same language, I'm not even sure we're the same species,'' she said, eyeing an empty table on the deck. ''Want to sit outside?''

''Good idea. As long as there's a table in the shade.''

It was a seat-yourself establishment, so they walked through the semicrowded restaurant, pushed through the double glass doors and took a table under a huge umbrella.

''I want French fries,'' Kendra announced as a young brunette waitress passed with a plate loaded with them.

''You can have fries with your burger,'' Sara said, ''but how about a pit stop first.''

Kendra hopped down from her chair so she could do her hands-on-hip routine. ''I don't need to go now.''

''Well, then you can just stay here with Mr. Nat.''

Sara waited until the waitress took their order, then excused herself. But her mood switched as she stepped back into the coolness of the restaurant, and she had the unsettling feeling that someone was watching her. She scanned the room, but no one was staring or seemed even vaguely suspicious.

The rest rooms were in the back, down a narrow hall and past the phone booths. The creepy feeling stayed with her, even though she knew it was ludicrous.

The bathroom had three stalls. No waiting. Actually, the room was empty. She stepped into the back stall and covered the seat with the sheet of protecting paper from the dispenser. She heard the heavy rest room door creak open as she lifted her skirt and slipped her panties down.

And then she saw the feet, standing right in front of her stall. Men's shoes. Dark brown leather. With brown shoelaces. "Troublemaker Sara Thomas. You never could just do as you were told, could you?"

Chapter Thirteen

Panic and adrenaline hit in a rush, clouding Sara's mind and then clearing it in a matter of heartbeats. She grabbed the lock, holding it tight while she yanked up her panties and tried to recall anything she'd ever heard about self defense.

Scream and flee. But if she screamed the guy would probably silence her forever with big meaty hands around her throat. And there was no way to flee, no way to get past him. But the heartbeats stretched into seconds, and he hadn't said more or tried to yank the door from her grip.

"Why are you doing this? Why are you tormenting me?"

"Because you don't listen. You were warned to keep quiet, but you just keep butting in."

"I haven't said anything. I don't know anything."

"You talked to the sheriff."

"Just to tell him I don't know about the babies buried in the wall. How would I?"

"Don't trifle with me. This is your last warning. Say one more word, and that little redheaded girl out there playing on the deck will be given her own grave."

Sara's stomach rolled and pitched, but the dread spiraled into fury. She gathered all her strength and shoved her shoulder into the door, hoping to slam it into the man's body, but it held tight and sent an excruciating jab of pain down her arm and her spine.

"You rotten sonofabitch. You touch my daughter and I'll find a way to make you pay. Do you hear me? I'll claw your heart out with my bare hands."

"Get the hell out of Georgia, Sara, and do it now. Or the girl is dead."

She heard his receding footsteps. She shoved the door again, but apparently he'd wedged something in it and it was stuck tight. Falling to the tile floor, she scooted beneath the stall and ran to the door. But by the time she got there, the man in the brown dress shoes had disappeared.

She slammed through the door of the men's room. Someone was at the urinal—wearing sneakers—his back to the door.

"Did a man just run in here?"

When he turned she could see that he was only a teenager. "No. I'm the only one in here," he said, zipping his fly.

She didn't waste time with an apology, just ducked out and rushed to the restaurant. No sign of the man, though all she knew him by was his shoes. Brown dress shoes with laces.

She checked out shoes as she walked through the restaurant and back to the deck, but she knew the man was gone. He'd already done what he'd come to do. Threatened not just her this time, but Kendra.

Murder. This morning when she'd talked to Nat, it had seemed something only a psycho or a person gone totally mad would be capable of. Now she knew that anyone was capable of it if the motivation were right. Because when he threatened Kendra she could have killed that man and never looked back.

Sara started to the table where Nat and Kendra were sipping soft drinks and looking at plastic menus. She stopped at a table that hadn't been cleared and yanked off a handful of paper towels. "Why don't you take these and throw them in that trash can over there?" Sara said, handing the wad of towels to Kendra.

Kendra hopped out of her chair, eager to have an excuse to wander from the table.

Sara touched Nat's shoulder. "He was here. In the ladies' room."

"Who was here?"

"The man who's been making the threats."

Nat went from halfway relaxed to livid. "Did he touch you?"

"No. He just talked." She explained the situation without taking her eyes off Kendra who'd stopped to talk to a grandmotherly woman at a nearby table.

"I shouldn't have let you out of my sight."

"You can't follow me every time I go to the bathroom, Nat. But I've had it."

"You can't be thinking of running away."

"No. I did that years ago. It doesn't work. You can't run from Meyers Bickham. It's like a cancerous growth that defies all treatment. But I will *not* let my daughter fall victim to that place or to a psychopath."

"Then we have to go after him, not wait for him to sneak around like the cowardly skunk that he is."

"You asked if I'd go back to Meyers Bickham. I'm ready to go now."

"I think we should pay a call on Dr. Abigail Hoyt Harrington first."

"They may not even be one and the same."

"They are. I didn't get a chance to tell you earlier, but Bob verified when he called that Dr. Harrington was the doctor on record during the first two years you were at the orphanage."

"It's not likely she'd remember the details of a young girl's nightmares for twenty years."

"But she might remember something that you don't."

"Then let's call her right now."

THE MEETING with Dr. Abigail Harrington was set for five o'clock the following afternoon. Only this time, Sara was not leaving Kendra with Dorinda. They'd have to drive all the way to Atlanta and she wanted Kendra with her or Nat every second.

"We're almost back to your house, Mr. Nat," Kendra piped from the back seat.

"How do you know that?"

"'Cause I saw that bridge we always cross."

"You're right," Nat said. "The next road is Delringer."

"Can we go swimming when we get there?"

"Later," Sara answered. "I have some things to take care of first."

"I was talking to Mr. Nat," Kendra reminded her.

"Sorry, Kendra," Nat said. "I've got work to do, too."

Five minutes later they pulled into the dirt drive in front of the rambling old house, but their plans for work would have to wait. A squad car was parked in the grass under the trees and Sheriff Troy Wesley was leaning against it, scowling.

"Looks like we have company," Nat said.

Sara only groaned as she climbed from the coolness of the van to the hot steam of a Georgia summer afternoon that she was sure was about to get hotter.

"Let's go check on Mackie," Sara said, rushing Kendra past the waiting sheriff and into the house.

"I want to talk to the policeman."

"Not now, sweetie. I think he's here on business."

"We didn't do anything wrong."

"I'm sure he just wants to talk to Nat."

Blake stood in the living room, swigging down a canned soft drink. He wiped his mouth on the back of his sleeve as Sara shut the door behind them. "Guess you saw the sheriff," he said.

"Nat's talking to him."

"I invited him in after he showed me his badge and everything, but he said he'd rather wait outside."

"How long has he been here?"

"About fifteen minutes."

"Mommy, he won't stop licking me," Kendra squealed.

"If you don't want Mackie to lick you, don't roll on the floor with him. And be careful of his hurt paw."

"I think he missed me while I was getting the gold."

"I'm sure he did." Sara checked Mackie's paw. The bandage showed signs of serious chewing, but it was still in place. The dog was doing a lot better than she was right now. "Can you keep an eye on Kendra for a few minutes, Blake?"

"Sure."

"Can I have a soft drink, too, Mommy?"

"How about a juice pack?"

"Okay."

"I'll get it," Blake said.

Sara murmured a hurried thanks and scooted out the front door. The sheriff and Nat were still standing by the squad car. Neither the sheriff nor Nat seemed to notice as she joined them. They were too deep into their verbal confrontation.

"I know all about you, Nat Sanderson. You didn't dupe me the way you have these folks that live around here."

"So you checked out my past. Nice to know you have a few investigating skills."

"I've got a damn sight more than a few and I don't need you or the FBI interfering in my case."

"Apparently that's not what the state attorney general thinks."

"He wasn't worried none about me or those dead babies until you started calling everyone you know at the Bureau."

"I didn't exactly get into this mess uninvited," Nat reminded him.

"Yeah, well banging your neighbor lady ain't reason enough to go messing up my case."

Nat's muscles tensed and for a second Sara was sure Nat was going to punch the sheriff. She rushed down the steps and grabbed his arm before he landed in jail.

"I don't see how who I *bang* or don't bang fits into the investigation, Sheriff," Sara said. "I'd think you'd welcome the help of the FBI since you don't appear to be making any headway."

"I'm making plenty of headway. I'm just not reporting it to you."

"Have you identified the bodies?"

"The case is confidential."

"So exactly why are you out here?" Nat asked.

"I'm just warning you to stay out of this, that's all. I'm trying to do my job and now I got some know-it-all bureaucrats that don't know nothing about North Georgia trying to tell me how to do it."

"The way I see it, that's your problem," Nat said. "Mine is keeping Sara safe and I'll do whatever it takes to do that."

"Then you might want to do a little investigating into the woman you're so fired up to protect. Find out just what kind of saint Sara Thomas was when she ran off from the orphanage and went to live on the streets at fifteen."

"It's Sara Murdoch," she corrected him, wishing she could belt him one herself now.

"I know all I need to know about Sara. And if you've said all you've come to say, then you can cut out any time."

"I'm leaving, but I meant what I said. Stay out of this, Nat. I'm not sure what we're up against here, and I don't want to see Sara or any other innocent people getting hurt over some kids who've been buried for twenty years."

Sara stood beside Nat as Troy gunned the engine and took off, spraying a sheet of mud behind him.

Nat muttered a string of curses, using them all as adjectives in front of Sheriff Wesley's name.

"He was right about one thing," Sara admitted. "I wasn't a saint during those years. I made my living by..."

"You don't need to explain that to me, Sara. I'm not helping you because I think you're some lily-white virgin. Whatever you did, you had your reasons."

"And it wouldn't matter to you if I'd been a hooker?"

"It wouldn't change who you are now and unless you left some dead bodies lying in your wake, you can't top me."

"Well, I wasn't a hooker. Would have starved to death if I'd tried it. I wore thick glasses and was so scrawny even the homeless kids on the streets gave me food."

"You filled out nicely," he said, resting his hand on her butt as they climbed the stairs together.

"Thank you. So what had the sheriff so pissed off?"

"Beats me, except that he doesn't like that the FBI's having further forensic testing done on the bodies and finding evidence he apparently overlooked."

"So he's afraid people will find out he's incompetent."

"Sounds that way," Nat agreed.

"You said earlier you thought this would all be over soon. What prompted that comment?"

"They found out who was in charge of funneling the money from the state to the orphanage."

"Who?"

"Judge Cary Arnold, only, of course he wasn't a judge back then."

"Are they going to question him?"

"I'm sure they are."

Sara tried to think positive as they walked back

inside the house, but even if the judge had shuffled funds twenty years ago she couldn't imagine a man of his stature replacing doll heads with skulls or threatening her in the ladies' rest room.

When the screen door squeaked open, it echoed in her mind like the cries of a ghost baby. And the threat made by the man in the bathroom seared into her brain.

I'm trying, ghost baby. I am. Just help me keep them away from Kendra.

IT WAS NEARLY ten o'clock, but Nat was still at the kitchen table poring over forms and reports and making notations in a spiral notebook. "I'm going to go buy a computer. Half of the data I need could be downloaded from the Internet if I had access."

"Listen to you. It's hard to believe you're the same reclusive apple grower I met a little over a week ago."

"It was shaving the beard that did it."

"It's getting back into criminal investigation that did it," she argued. "You thrive on it."

"I just wish I had some authority instead of having to sit in the dugout and watch the game."

"Have you thought of going back to work with the FBI?"

"Sure, me and my bum leg." He reached down and rubbed his thigh as if mentioning it caused it to ache. "I'd be lucky to get a desk job."

"But you'd be out of the huddle."

"The dugout. Not the huddle. Being out of the huddle is not good."

"Let's go back to desks. I understand those better. Would a desk job be all that bad?"

He grabbed her hand and tugged her onto his lap. "Let's forget me." He stroked her back with the flat of his hand, then moved to the base of her neck and let his fingers tangle in her hair. "You were great today. Really great."

"Because I didn't fall apart."

"Didn't even come close. Tough as a mother grizzly protecting her cub."

"If I had gotten my hands on him I think I could have stuffed him into that toilet headfirst."

"Would have just dirtied up the sewer system."

"Do you think it could have been Judge Arnold?"

"I doubt it. Might have been someone he paid to do his dirty work. But then, you never know what some people will sink to."

"Especially a man who'd let babies be fed to the rats."

He massaged her shoulders, then kissed her on the back of the neck. "You should probably go to bed and try to get some sleep. You have to be tired after a day like this."

"Are you going to bed?"

"In a while."

So that was how it would be. Just crawl into her bed and pretend that her body didn't ache for his, that in spite of everything going wrong in her life she didn't want his kiss so badly she could taste it.

But she couldn't pretend. It wasn't her way. "Does that mean that you don't want to make love with me tonight?"

"Is that what you think?"

"I don't know what to think. That's why I'm asking."

He buried his face in her hair and held her, not

saying a word. She'd never been sure of herself with men. The only real relationship she'd ever been in was with Steven and it had gone bad right after the wedding.

"I want to make love with you, Sara. How could I not? I even considered picking you up at one point this afternoon, carrying you off to the shed and ravaging you. How's that for a reclusive apple grower?"

"But you didn't."

"The timing doesn't seem right."

"Why? Nat, I'm so tired of graves and dead babies and talk of depravity. Make love with me and make the ugliness disappear if only for a few minutes."

"If it was just that easy."

"It is easy, Nat. I'm not asking for any kind of promises or commitments. I had those. It turned out they didn't mean a thing."

"Oh, Sara. You make this so hard. When this is over I'll make love with you every morning and every night and show up for afternoon delight if you want. But right now, I've got to stay in control and concentrate on keeping you safe. It was bad enough that I almost slugged Wesley this afternoon for his comments about you. If I had, I'd be in jail tonight and not doing you a damn bit of good."

"Would it have been any different if we hadn't made love?"

"I don't know. I just know that the unwritten code of a bodyguard is to never become so emotionally involved that your judgment is clouded."

And he'd made that mistake before, become involved with a woman and lost his perspective. She understood his fear and his pain, but they were already involved and she didn't see how making love could possibly make anything worse.

"I'm not Maria, Nat. I'm not beautiful or exotic and I don't have any hidden agenda." She put her arms around him and rested her head on his shoulder, putting her lips close to his ear. "I'm just plain Sara, and I need you to hold me in your arms and make me believe that there's still something right in the world."

"You are far from plain, Sara Murdoch. You are the most exasperating, most fascinating, most intriguing woman I have ever been seduced by." He kissed the tip of her nose. "Now get out of here before I forget everything in that speech I just gave and make love to you right here on the kitchen table."

"You think I'm seductive?"

"Without a doubt."

"That's not the same as making love to me, but it's close."

"Not doing a hell of a lot for me."

She walked to the door, swaying her hips as if she really were some femme fatale and not the gangly, wild-haired woman she knew she was. "My door will be unlocked if you change your mind."

"Redheaded hussy."

"You silver-tongued devil."

But the good mood lasted only until the screech of an owl attacked the silence of the night. She went to the window and stared out at the shadows creeping through the moonlight. Almost a full moon.

The owl screeched again, but this time he was farther away and sounded like a baby crying. She shivered, then went to bed and crawled under the covers.

Images from the old nightmare tumbled in her mind. The dark basement. The parade.

Hold on tight.

For a second she thought she'd screamed, but it was only the owl, swooping through the trees, his cries echoing through the night and through her mind as if the ghosts had sent him to find her.

She closed her eyes and willed the images to disappear, but instead they started the parade. Dark, frightening figures marching though her mind.

Her door squeaked open and she sat up in bed as if she'd been shot. Nat stepped inside.

"I can't do it, Sara. I just can't stay away."

She opened her arms and he crawled inside them. And the ghosts tiptoed away. She knew they'd be back. They always came back. Meyers Bickham had long ago laid claim to her soul, but for now Nat held her heart in his hands.

SARA LAY AWAKE long after the lovemaking, lying in the spot where Nat had been, imagining that he was still there and that she was cuddled in his arms. Not that it had been a wham-bammer.

He'd taken his time, made love to every inch of her and let her return the favor, but they both agreed that it would be too confusing for Kendra if she woke in the night, trotted into Sara's room and found Nat in her mother's bed.

Sara reached down and touched herself where Nat had entered her and imagined it was him touching her again. Their lovemaking was so new that each touch and kiss was like discovering a treasure. Finding out what made him writhe in anticipation, what made him moan in pleasure, what made him suck in his breath.

She was finding out about herself, too. That she loved Nat's trailing kisses down her abdomen, loved the feel of his breath on her skin, the way it tickled when his hair brushed her nipples.

Caught up in a living hell and yet falling madly in love with someone she'd known such a short time seemed impossible. Yet it seemed as natural as breathing. The passion fed on the danger, drew from its intensity and exploded the way she couldn't let the fear.

She didn't know what would happen between her and Nat when this was over, when he no longer felt the pull of intrigue and the zeal for keeping her and Kendra safe, but for now she didn't want to even think of getting through this without him.

She closed her eyes, but in the darkness the desire and passion took on surreal qualities, then slowly slipped into the dread that had hit her today when the brown shoes had come into view.

She trembled and pulled the covers higher, as the shoes changed to rats, big gray rats that darted through the beam of her flashlight. She hovered against the wall of the basement, but she had to be brave. She was the oldest. She'd talked them into this. She couldn't let them see how frightened she was.

"I don't like it down here. It's too scary."

"It's not scary. It's exciting."

"We're going to get in trouble."

"What was that noise?"

"Rats. They're everywhere."

"They're more afraid of us than we are of them."

"Not as afraid as I am, I bet."

"Let's play a game. Let's play 'I Wish.'"

Someone giggled. And then everyone giggled, and giggled and giggled. But the rats just kept coming.

"The noise is behind us. It's coming out of the wall."

"It's a baby. A ghost baby."

No one was giggling now.

"Let's hold hands. Hold on very tight. Don't let the ghost break the circle. Ghosts can't break a circle of friends."

Sara's hands hurt. She was holding on so tight. But the baby ghost kept crying. And crying. And crying.

Sara jerked awake, sitting up straight in bed and slapping at the rats. Only there were no rats. It was the nightmare. And Mackie barking.

He lets me know the second someone's around.

Sara threw her feet over the side of the bed and raced to Nat's door. He was already up and wiggling into this jeans in only the light of the moon filtering through the windows.

"Do you think there's someone out there?"

"I hope so."

He turned and picked up two pistols from the table beside him. "This is loaded. If someone besides me comes through that door, shoot him."

She took the gun and the fear hit again, like suffocating smoke filling her lungs. "Where will you be?"

"Outside. Lock the door behind me and leave the lights off."

"You can't go out there alone."

He looked at her as if she were speaking a language he didn't understand.

"I have Mackie."

And then he was gone. And she was left with a gun she couldn't bear to touch, her daughter sleeping in the room down the hall and who knows what in the yard outside the rambling farmhouse.

Chapter Fourteen

Sara paced the house, checking locks on doors and windows and peeking in on Kendra, terrifying possibilities flitting through her mind like some horror flick on fast forward. Her eyes had adjusted to the darkness now and she could see the outlines of trees. But there was no sign of Mackie and no sign of Nat.

She glanced at the clock over the kitchen table a hundred times in the next half hour. The hands seemed to drag, moving slower and slower until she finally heard footsteps on the back steps.

Nat. It had to be Nat. But what if it wasn't? All of a sudden, the pistol felt like a dead weight in her hand, straining her muscles, as she fit her finger on the trigger.

"Nat. Is that you?"

"It's me, Sara. You can put down the gun. Everything's fine. Unlock the door."

She lay the pistol on the table and rushed to the door. Her fingers were shaking as she turned the key and yanked the heavy wooden door open. Mackie trotted inside, nuzzling her leg as she fell into Nat's arms.

"Oh, Nat, I'm so glad it was nothing."

"It was something."

"What do you mean?"

"Someone's been in the shed. He'd taken the scythe off the hook."

"Where is he now?"

"Out of here. I went running after Mackie and saw the lights of a vehicle hightailing it down the old logging road."

"Mackie must have frightened him off."

"No doubt about it. I think he also bit a plug out of the guy. There's blood on the floor of the shed. Probably would have had him down on the ground and waiting for me if he didn't have that sore paw."

"Do you think he was going to attack us with a scythe?"

"I doubt he came here unarmed."

"But he didn't shoot Mackie."

"A gunshot would have alerted us even faster than barking. He was probably going to shut Mackie up with a swish of the scythe."

"What do we do now? We can't just go to sleep."

"You can."

"But Nat, you can't stay up all night and day."

"I'll sleep in the kitchen chair with Mackie right beside me, and if there's any movement outside, he'll wake me, won't you, boy?"

Mackie wagged his tail to seal the deal.

"Why not call the local sheriff?"

"And have him do what? Drive around town and look for some guy who's already long gone or else fits in around here so well, the sheriff wouldn't suspect him if they shared the same bar stool?"

"This has to stop, Nat. We can't go on like this. We can't."

"I agree."

When she finally left Nat's arms, she went to Mackie who'd sprawled under the kitchen chair where Nat usually sat.

"I'm glad you bit him, Mackie," she said, running her fingers across his coat and scratching his ears. "I hope you bit him hard. And I hope he bled all over a pair of brown shoes."

"I THINK I'll call the hospital again," Sara said as they sat in deadlocked Atlanta traffic.

"We're not late for the appointment yet."

"No, I mean call the hospital in Columbus and check on Raye Ann."

"Might as well. We're going nowhere fast here."

"Guess it's been awhile since you've dealt with traffic," she said.

"Yeah, especially with a kid in the back seat."

"How does that change things?"

"Have to scale down my coping language."

"So that's why you keep opening and closing your mouth with nothing coming out. I thought you were having a seizure."

Small talk, but it was a farce. There was no getting past the strain now. The shed and the area around the house had been crawling with FBI agents this morning, looking for clues and gathering blood samples for DNA testing. But Nat still insisted things were moving fast and this would be over soon.

The FBI was checking out the orphanage records, trying to determine where each of the babies admitted to the orphanage during Sara's stay had actually wound up. They'd already found one gaping discrepancy that Sara was certain she would never have learned about if Nat wasn't a former agent and hadn't been working with them so closely on this case. There was no doubt that Bob Eggars trusted him implicitly.

According to adoption records, one severely handicapped baby had been adopted by a couple in Macon, Georgia. Only the alleged adoptive family had never existed. Nat was already speculating that the handicapped infant could be one of the bodies that had been buried in the basement wall. It was almost too gory for Sara to think about without getting nauseous.

Sara turned to check on Kendra. She was holding her stuffed bear and nodding. She never took naps at home anymore, but in a car she almost always drifted off.

Traffic started creeping along again and Sara punched in the now familiar number, hoping this time she'd get someone who had time to fill her in on Raye Ann's progress.

"ICU. Can I help you?"

"This is Sara Murdoch and I'm calling to see if I can get an update on Raye Ann Jackson."

"Oh, Mrs. Murdoch. I'm glad you called. I was just about to go look up your phone number."

Sara sucked in a breath through gritted teeth. "Is something wrong?"

"No. It's good news. Raye Ann came out of the coma. She didn't say but a few words but she nodded and shook her head in response to the doctor's questions. Even got the number of fingers he was holding up right. We're all thrilled."

"Can I talk to her?"

"She's resting now, but she asked for you."

"Really? Did you tell her I'd called every day?"

"I did. She's had lots of calls from friends, but you were the only one she asked about. It might be good if you came in to see her later. You couldn't stay long, but seeing a familiar face might do her good."

"I'll try. How late can she have visitors tonight?"

"The last scheduled visitation is at eight, but if you get here later, ask for Janice. I'll let you in for a few minutes. I think you'd be better than medicine for Raye Ann, help her get grounded in reality after being out of it for so long."

Sara wasn't even certain she was grounded in reality anymore, but she would like to see Raye Ann. "Thanks. And thanks for the good news."

"I'm just glad I had some for a change."

"Me, too. Very glad."

"You look pleased," Nat said, when she'd broken the connection.

"Raye Ann's regained consciousness."

"Terrific. And hopefully she'll be able to give a good description of her attacker."

"I hadn't even thought of that. How do you feel about driving over there after we leave the hospital?"

"It's fine with me, if you're up to it."

"I am. We'll make a stop for chicken nuggets first and let Kendra have some playtime."

The traffic started to move and Sara spotted the hospital just ahead.

"Looks like we'll make the appointment right on schedule," Nat said.

"Good. It might just be relief from getting a bit of good news, but I think Raye Ann's progress is an omen that the meeting with Dr. Harrington will go well.''

''I wish I could be there when you talk to her.''

''I know, but I'd rather you stay outside with Kendra. And don't worry. I can handle it.'' She crossed her fingers as she made that pronouncement, a little added help for the omen.

''RIGHT THIS WAY, Mrs. Murdoch.''

Sara handed Nat the phone as she got up to follow the young nurse in the blue print lab coat.

Nat squeezed her hand. ''Kendra and I will be right here in the waiting room. If you change your mind and want me to come in with you, just let me know.''

She nodded, but she wouldn't change her mind, the same way she hadn't changed it when Nat had wanted her to leave Kendra with Henry and Dorinda so he could be with her when she talked to the doctor.

She wanted her daughter safe and protected, not only from harm but from the curse of Meyers Bickham. Which meant Kendra definitely didn't need to hear Sara discuss old nightmares with a busy pediatrician who probably didn't even remember her.

The doors to the examining rooms were all closed and the halls were empty, eerily quiet except for the echoes of their footsteps on the tiled floor. The biting odor of disinfectant was strong but not so much that it obscured the fragrance of a flowery perfume or the smell of old coffee that wafted from the end of the hall.

''Have a seat,'' the nurse said, stopping at the one

door that was open. "The doctor will be with you in a minute."

"Thanks."

The office was more luxurious than Sara had expected, though it still had all the trappings of a typical doctor's office. Framed diplomas and honors covered the wall behind the massive desk. The words Meyers Bickham seemed to leap out at her, and she walked behind the desk to get a closer look at the Certificate of Appreciation the orphanage had bestowed on her nineteen years earlier. For dedication and service to children forgotten by the world.

"Hello, Sara."

The voice reached inside Sara, found old memories and seemed to gather them into a knot just under her rib cage. She turned and stared at the woman who'd stepped to the door. It had been almost two decades, but Sara would have recognized her if she'd seen her on the street. Her hair was the same soft brown, mixed shades, as if it had been painted by an artist. Her skin was flawless, her lips curved in a welcoming smile.

"I don't know if you remember me," Sara said, "but I was one of the forgotten children of the world who lived at Meyers Bickham."

"Of course I remember you. You were one scared little girl, terrified by nightmares and angry at your mother for dying and leaving you all alone."

"You remember those days better than I do."

"You were a little girl. I was a grown-up intern thrilled to be earning money at my new profession." Dr. Harrington closed the door behind her and walked to her leather chair behind the massive desk. "Have a seat, Sara, and tell me how you've been."

Sara sat in one of the two chairs facing the doctor's desk. "I'm a history professor in Columbus and I have an adorable daughter, who'll be five this summer."

"Sounds as if you've come a long way. It's always good to hear that about a kid who got a rotten deal from life."

"I've done well, but the nightmares are still with me," Sara said. "In a way that's why I'm here. Not that I expect you to deal with them. I'd just like to know if you remember what they were like initially. I know it's not likely at this late date, but…"

"I remember them," Dr. Harrington said. "At least the basic structure of them. Tell me what you remember of the nightmares and I'll see if that fits with my recollection."

"They change, but a few things seem to stay constant."

"Which illusions were lasting?"

"The rats. Really big rats."

"I can understand that. There were rats there. I insisted they have the place exterminated, but it never seemed to completely solve the problem. The boys who were brave enough to sneak into the basement used to spread tales that the rats were so thick down there that you couldn't take two steps without stepping on one. I was never brave enough to see if they were telling the truth." Dr. Harrington smiled, and Sara felt some of the tension seep from her muscles.

"Would you like some hot tea or coffee? The coffee's rather stale by this point in the day, but I can make some fresh."

"No, I'm fine," Sara said.

"Then go on. What else do you see in the nightmares?"

"There's some kind of parade. A somber parade. The person in front is carrying a lantern and someone else has a laundry basket."

Sara told as much as she could remember, and the doctor pressed her for even more details.

"Do you think it's possible I was really in the basement and saw something like that?"

"I seriously doubt it, Sara. You'd just lost your mother and been moved to a strange environment. You were surrounded by strangers you didn't trust and terrified of everything. I can't imagine that you'd have ever sneaked into that musty basement. I'm not even sure the older boys went down there. I always suspected they just made up the stories to torment the girls and younger kids."

"Do you remember if I talked about a parade or a procession back then?"

"Most of your nightmares had clear anxiety connections. Being thrown into the basement. Seeing your mother but not being able to catch up with her. Having friends who you tried to hold on to, but they kept running away. But the idea of a procession could stem from your mother's funeral. You could have transposed some of those memories into fragments of your nightmares."

The longer they talked, the more Sara began to doubt that the nightmares had any connection to reality at all except as a way to deal with the anxiety she'd been feeling at the time. Maybe they were still her coping mechanism.

"I seem to remember that you gave me something

to help control the nightmares. Do you know what I might have taken?''

"I couldn't name the drug, but I'm sure it was an antianxiety medication. Treatment has changed over the years, so whatever I used has probably been dramatically improved upon by now.''

"There is one other thing,'' Sara said. "Most of the dreams are accompanied by the sound of a baby crying. In the nightmare, I think it's a ghost baby.''

"Crying babies. Now that's a nightmare I can relate to.'' The doctor leaned back in her chair and tented her hands. "I don't mean to make light of it, but I'm not surprised that you'd be haunted by that. There were always so many babies at Meyers Bickham that I don't think there was ever a time when there wasn't at least one baby crying, usually more than one.''

"I don't remember there being that many babies there at any one time.''

"It always seemed like a lot to me when I was taking care of them. But then perhaps that's because I was an intern and always tired from the work I did at the hospital during the day. Meyers Bickham was my moonlighting job. I was out there every weekend and whenever there was an emergency. Of course, if it was a real emergency, the children were taken to a hospital.''

"But you spent a lot of time with me, at least that's how I remember it.''

"I think I identified with you, Sara. You see, my mother died when I was only nine. I wasn't sent to an orphanage but I went to live with an aunt and uncle who didn't really want me. And I did just as you did. Pretended to be brave, kept the pain inside and released the fear and anxiety through terrifying nightmares.''

They talked awhile longer, but even though the doctor didn't seem to be in a rush, Sara knew that she'd taken up enough of her time. She slid her handbag back across her shoulder and scooted to the edge of her chair. ''I appreciate your seeing me.''

''I hope I was at least a little bit helpful.''

''You were, but I'm still confused about a lot of things.'' She glanced at her watch. ''I better go now. I have a friend in a hospital in Columbus and I'm going to try and see her tonight.''

''Are you going there now?''

''Yes.''

''Drive carefully,'' Dr. Harrington said, walking with Sara to the door. ''I'm glad you came in. It's nice to see one of my kids grow into such a smart, attractive young lady.''

''Not so young anymore. I'm thirty.''

''Ah, yes. I remember it well.''

They shook hands and Sara let herself out, following the long hallway back to Nat—without any real answers.

KENDRA HAD REVIVED after her nap and was wound up after her stop for chicken nuggets and play on the brightly colored plastic play equipment. As always she made immediate friends with the other kids and would have stayed and played for hours if they'd let her.

But it was just over a hundred miles to Columbus and then they'd have the long drive back to the apple orchard. They headed south on I-85, with a just a quick call to Henry, who was looking in on the place and on Mackie today. All was apparently quiet on the home front and there was no new news from the FBI.

Nat flicked on the radio just past Lagrange, just in time to hear a special news bulletin that Judge Cary Arnold had been shot and killed in his own garage as he'd arrived home from work during an apparent burglary attempt.

"Did you hear that?" Sara asked, doubting her own ears.

"Loud and clear."

"This has to be connected with the investigation. What do you think it means?" Sara kept her voice low so that she didn't steal Kendra's attention from the tape of children's songs she was listening to in the back seat."

"Maybe you're not the only one someone's trying to keep quiet."

It hit her again how lucky she was to be alive. She reached over and laid her hand on Nat's thigh. "It's nice to have a bodyguard."

"And it's good motivation to keep me at the top of my game."

"You're always at the top of your game. But the judge was a major suspect. What will that do to the investigation?"

"Throw a few more kinks in it, that's for sure."

"You know I hate to admit I could be wrong, Nat, but it's starting to look more and more like there's something far more sinister than just misuse of funds going on here."

"You mean something like m-u-r-d-e-r?"

"Yeah, but I haven't admitted it yet. I'm just closer than I was."

"And this is one time I'd love to be proven wrong."

IT WAS 8:32 p.m. when they arrived at the Columbus Hospital where Raye Ann was a patient. Just after the end of visiting time in the ICU, but, true to her word, Janice welcomed Sara and took her to Raye Ann's bed.

"I can't let you stay but a few minutes," Janice said. "She tires easily."

Sara tried to hide her dismay at seeing the usually vivacious older woman pale and hooked up to a disturbing array of lifesaving tubes. But Raye Ann's eyes were open and she was alert.

"I'm glad you're better," Sara said, placing her hand on Raye Ann's."

"Hit on the head."

"I heard about it. I'm sorry. I thought the apartment was safe."

"Not your fault."

Her words were slightly slurred and little more than a whisper.

"How's the cabin?"

No time to tell her it had burned to the ground or that Sara and Kendra were barely staying one step away from what might be the same man who had attacked her. "It's nice in the mountains."

"Good."

Raye Ann took a deep breath.

"Hope they find my attacker."

Sara hesitated. She hadn't planned to bring up the subject of the beating for fear of upsetting Raye Ann, but since she was talking about it, there was no reason to avoid the subject.

"Can you describe him?"

"Had on a ski mask." Raye Ann wet her lips with her tongue. "Need some water."

Sara poured some water from the pitcher on the bedside table and lifted the glass, putting the straw to Raye Ann's lips. She took a few sips then indicated she'd had enough.

"Did you see his shoes?"

"When he hit me. I fell and he kicked me. Hard. They were brown. With ties. Expensive. The freakin' bastard."

"The freakin' bastard," Sara agreed as anger swelled inside her. It had to be the same man who'd accosted her in the ladies' room. He wanted to frighten Sara to keep her from talking, but he'd attacked Raye Ann for no reason except that she was Sara's friend. And he would try to hurt Kendra.

"They'll find him, Raye Ann."

"I hope so."

They talked a minute more before the nurse said it was time for Sara to leave. She hurried back to the waiting room, anxious to see Nat and tell him what Raye Ann had said. She wondered if the man with the brown shoes was on the run right now, with a dog bite on his leg.

"BROWN SHOES DON'T PROVE we're talking about the same man," Nat said, "but it does make it more likely. I'd like to pass that on to Bob and also let him know that Raye Ann's attacker wore a ski mask. So far the doctors haven't let the police in to talk to her."

"Then even the FBI thinks her attack might not have been a foiled burglary attempt?"

"They're checking all angles."

Sara handed Nat the phone so that he could make the call.

"I'm ready to go, Mommy."

"I'm sure you are, sweetie. We'll only be a few minutes. Would you like to get some ice cream before we drive home?"

"Yes. Can I have a cone?"

"I don't see why not. As soon as Nat's off the phone we'll go find an ice-cream shop." And hopefully after that, Kendra would fall asleep in the car and sleep the three plus hour drive back to Nat's.

Nat punched in the number, then moved to the back corner of the waiting room to get a little privacy.

Kendra tugged from her grasp and scooted over to stand by a uniformed cop who was standing by the door.

"Do you shoot people with your gun?"

"Not so far. How old are you?"

"Four, but I'm almost five."

Leave it to Kendra to make friends with a cop.

"Are you Sara Murdoch?"

Sara turned to the male nurse who'd appeared at her side."

"Yes."

"Dr. Purdue would like to see you for a few minutes before you leave."

"Dr. Purdue?"

"Raye Ann Jackson's doctor."

"Is something wrong?"

He didn't answer the question, but she could tell that there was. He wore that glum expression that people always had when they had bad news to tell you.

"I'm not certain what he wants to talk to you

about. He just heard that you'd been in to see Raye
Ann and asked me to see if you were still here.''

"Where is he?"

"In his office. I'll take you there."

"I have to wait for my friend to get off the phone
so he can watch my..."

She looked around for Kendra. The cop was no
longer by the door. And Kendra was nowhere in
sight.

Chapter Fifteen

Sara scanned the room. She'd only taken her eyes off Kendra for a second. She had to be here. Only she wasn't. *She was not in this room.*

The door to the hallway was open and Sara rushed through it, feeling as if she might literally fold like a deck of cards at any second. But the policeman was standing a few feet away, near an elevator leaning against a wheelchair and staring at the door. He'd surely have seen Kendra if she'd left the room.

"Did my daughter come out that door?"

"Do I know your daughter?"

"You were talking to her just a few seconds ago. Red hair. She's only four years old."

"She went this way. I'll help you find her."

"Is something wrong?" The nurse that had been talking to Sara had followed her into the hall and was right behind them pushing the wheelchair. He punched the button on the service elevator.

"My daughter. She was here a minute ago, and now she's gone."

"I think I know where she is," the cop said calmly as the elevator door slid open and an orderly got out and walked hurriedly past.

"Your daughter's fine, *Sara.*"

She knew something was dreadfully wrong the second he said her name. Her first impulse was to scream for Nat, but everything happened too fast. The policeman's hand was over her mouth and she felt the prick of a needle as it broke the skin in her right arm and plunged into her vein.

The men were on either side of her now, lifting her into the elevator. They shoved her into the wheelchair and buckled her in.

She heard the clang of the elevator. And then the world went black. She couldn't see anything, but she could hear the horrid, plaintive sound of the ghost baby crying for someone to help it.

"SORRY FOR THE WAIT, Nat. I was on the phone with the patrolman who found Cary Arnold's body."

"What's up with that?"

"I don't know any more than you do if you saw the news."

"Heard it on the radio."

"I'm sure it's related to the orphanage case. You were right on target with that. The adoption records are totally screwed up. But Arnold's not the only big news of the day."

"Anything you can tell me about?"

"Actually something I should warn you about. That sheriff who's handling the case, the one you've talked to a couple of times?"

"Sheriff Troy Wesley."

"That's the man. He worked at Meyers Bickham as a security guard twenty years ago."

"How'd you find that out? I didn't see his name anywhere in the list of employees I had."

"From one of the caretakers we questioned. She still lives in the area and knows Wesley. But, are you ready for this?"

"Hit me with it."

"The biggest contributor to his campaign fund when he was running for sheriff was Cary Arnold."

"That connects a few dots. My news is going to sound blasé after your day." Nat told him about Sara's visit with Raye Ann, scanning the room for her as he did. He knew she wouldn't have gone anywhere without telling him, but he sure as hell didn't see her.

"I've got to run, Bob."

"You sound upset. Is something wrong?"

"Shouldn't be. I'll talk to you later."

"Be careful."

"Yeah." Nat scanned the room again. It was full of people, couples, families with children, some teenagers. No one could have come in and abducted Sara and Kendra in a roomful of people. He would have been aware of any kind of commotion, would have heard her if she'd called his name. She'd probably taken Kendra to the bathroom.

His nervous system didn't buy that answer. He rushed back to where he'd left her and started questioning people at random.

"She left with a male nurse," a middle-aged woman said. "He came in and asked if she was Mrs. Murdoch and she left with him. He said her friend's doctor wanted to see her."

That had to be it. He'd rake her over the coals for leaving the room without telling him where she was going. He couldn't take this kind of stress. He checked the hallway. It was empty except for a couple of guys in green scrubs standing near the service elevator.

"Did you see a woman and a kid go by here?"

"Naw. Just walked up." The elevator doors slid open and they stepped in. Nat rushed down the hall to check the nearby ladies' room. Nothing. He went back to the ICU and began to question the nurses, panic hitting in hurricane-strength waves as he heard what he didn't want to hear. Raye Ann's doctor had left the hospital a couple of hours ago and wasn't due back until morning. And there were no male nurses on duty in the unit that night.

Nat rushed back into the hall and took the service elevator down to ground level, his mind skipping over possibilities, trying to piece together a reasonable scenario of how an abduction could have transpired.

The service elevator opened a few steps from an emergency exit. An easy escape for an abductor—or abductors. They could have just walked out that door to a waiting car. Sara and Kendra could be anywhere. Anywhere at all. And Nat had let it happen.

The old memories hit hard, and Nat literally stumbled backward at the impact to his mind and spirit. He saw the blood and the bodies and felt the sense of failure and horror as if it were happening all over again. Only this time it was Sara and Kendra that he'd failed.

An ambulance sped past, sirens blaring and lights flashing, jolting Nat back to his senses. He had to do something and do it now. Every second counted. He raced back to the parking lot. Sara's van was missing.

A guy rode up on a Harley and pulled it into a

parking space behind Nat. When the guy got off, Nat jumped on.

"Hey, man! Get off my bike."

"I gotta borrow it. My woman's in trouble, but you'll get it back. I promise you'll get it back."

The man reared back to punch him, and Nat pulled his gun. "Get out of my way. Now!"

The guy put up his hands and stepped back. "You need it that bad, you take it. Go get her."

And Nat was off, not even sure where he was going, but he had to find Sara, and he had to find her fast. And wherever she was, he was almost certain that Troy Wesley would be there, too.

SARA OPENED her eyes and tried to shake loose from the hold of a haze that covered her mind. Finally her vision cleared enough for her to see that she was riding in the back seat of a four-door sedan. Her feet and hands were bound tight with what looked like some kind of surgical tape.

"Where's my daughter? Where's Kendra?" she demanded, her tongue slapping around in her mouth like a slab of raw meat.

"Your daughter's fine, Sara. She's in good hands."

"Why are you doing this?"

"I'm just following orders, lady."

"You're not a cop, are you?"

"I can be anything I need to be." The man took off the police cap and yanked a dark brown wig from his head, leaving a disheveled mat of blond hair. "Same way I wasn't an FBI agent."

"You're not the man who came to the cabin."

"Sure I am." He unbuttoned his shirt and took out some kind of gauzy padding, then peeled off his dark eyebrows. Cheap theatrical makeup, but it had been convincing. "Just think of me as Agent Jack Trotter if you like. 'Course, I looked a bit different that day, too."

The driver glanced at her in the rearview mirror. The male nurse. The same guys who'd come to the cabin. She should have known, but it was all too bizarre.

The haze took over again, and her head lolled back against the headrest. It was the injection that was knocking her out. She had to fight it.

"How did you know I'd be at the hospital tonight?"

"Can't give away our little secrets," the pseudo nurse said. "But you did make it easy. We expected to have to ambush the three of you when you got to your van. But you just walked right into our hands."

"Yeah" the other guy added. "By the way, that's a cute, friendly daughter you have. Too bad you won't be around to see her grow up."

If Sara could have lifted her feet, she would have kicked him in the back of the head, but her arms and legs felt as if they'd been cast in cement, and things were starting to spin.

"Stop the car. I'm going to be sick."

"Not falling for that old trick, sweetheart."

"So whose…tricks did you…fall…." The words quit coming. She was capitulating, plunging into a cold, dark basement.

And there was nothing she could do to stop the fall.

NAT DROVE around Columbus, down back alleys, through motel parking lots, finding the worst spots in the worst sections of what was basically a very nice town. And he wasn't at this alone. There were cops and FBI agents not only in Columbus but all over Georgia and surrounding states heeding the APB, but no one had spotted Sara's van.

He was stopped in a desolate area behind an abandoned and crumbling building when the mobile rang. He grabbed it, praying it would be Sara. "Nat Sanderson."

"Mack Billings with the state police."

Nat knew from the sound of his voice the news was not good. "Did you find Sara and Kendra?"

"No, but we located the van, and a—"

"Just say it."

"There was a kid's shoe outside the car."

"That's it?"

"Pretty much. One small white sneaker and several sets of footprints. One of them belonged to a woman. And tire prints for two other cars."

"Where was this?"

"In the back corner of a mall parking lot in north Atlanta."

"I'd like the exact location." Nat scribbled down the address, though he knew it was a waste of time. They'd be long gone from there by now, same as they were long gone from Columbus. It had been two hours since they'd disappeared. They could be anywhere by now. Anywhere at all. Alive or...

No. If he started thinking that way he might as well find a hole to crawl into and die himself. A little more than a week, and he couldn't bear to think of life without Sara.

He started the engine of the stolen bike and headed

north. He needed a clue. A hint. Hell, he needed a huge freakin' break, and he and Sara were both long overdue.

SARA LURCHED forward as the car skidded to a stop. She kept fading in and out of the drug-induced trance, and she had no idea how long they'd been on the road or where they were right now.

The back door opened and the damp coolness of the night air collided with her clammy flesh.

"So nice to see you again, Sara."

"Dr. Harrington."

"Surprised to see me?"

"I don't understand."

"Oh, come now, Sara. With all the snooping you and Nat Sanderson have been doing, you should know everything about me by now."

"No. Why are you doing this?"

"What other choice did you give me?"

A nightmare. This was all a nightmare. She'd wake up in a few minutes, and she'd be back in Nat's comfortable old house.

Abigail stepped back from the car. "Take the tape off her feet and hands. If she tries anything, shoot her."

"Where is my daughter?"

"She's safe, for now. I have no reason to harm her."

"Is she afraid? Is she crying for me?"

"She's sleeping."

"You drugged her."

"Would you rather she be crying for you? What kind of mother are you, Sara Thomas?"

Sara tried to kick at the man who was yanking the

tape from her feet, but her muscles weren't cooperating.

"No need to make this difficult, Sara. It's all but over now."

Sara tried to fight the haziness. Things around her seemed to swell and shrink, changing shape and size and even color. The men were holding her, dragging her down a rocky hill. The moon was full, a huge ball, first silver, then bright blue, bouncing so close that she ducked once to keep it from hitting her.

The beam of someone's flashlight danced in front of them, in and out, in and out, burning holes in the dirt. And then she saw the orphanage. The old church. The big double doors that swallowed you when you walked inside them. The spire that pointed to heaven even though hell was in the basement with the rats and the crying babies.

The orphanage faded as quickly as it had appeared, replaced by a deep hole in the ground cluttered with broken bricks, leaves and pieces of broken lumber.

"There's your basement, Sara. Still full of rats. Hungry, hungry rats."

Someone shoved her and she staggered down the incline. And she was ten again, lonely, afraid and shivering in the darkness.

"Wait a minute. I heard that noise again," Jessica said, *"and it's not a rat."*

"I hear it, too. It's coming out of that wall."

"It's a baby. A ghost baby."

"Let's hold hands," Sara said.

They held hands, but the baby kept crying. And it didn't sound like a ghost at all.

"It's a baby."

"It's a ghost baby."

"I'm afraid. I want to go back to my room."

"Hold tight," Sara said. *"Hold on very tight in a circle. Ghosts can't break a circle of friends."*

The memories came back, clear as if it were all happening in real time. Jessica and Daphne were right beside her. The three of them had sneaked down to the basement to be together after lights out and that's when they'd heard the ghost baby crying in the wall. If only she'd remembered sooner, she and Nat could have looked for her friends, found out if they knew anything that could help.

Then she remembered more. Jessica and Daphne hadn't seen the procession. That had been another night.

"It's our last night together," Jessica said. *"I don't want to leave. I don't want a foster home. I want to stay with you two."*

"You can't stay with me," Daphne said. *"I won't be here. They don't want me here anymore. I'm going to the Grace Girls' Home, wherever that is. They'll probably hate me there. I won't have any friends."*

"And I'll be left here," Sara said. *"But I won't stay long. I'm going to run away."*

"Don't do it, Sara. They'll catch you and you'll be in so much trouble. Promise me you won't do it."

"I'm not afraid of those old caretakers. I'm not afraid of anything."

"You were afraid that night the ghost baby cried," Jessica reminded her.

"But she didn't run away," Daphne said. *"She made us stay and hold hands, and she was right. Nothing can break a circle of friends. Let's promise to be friends forever."*

"Listen, I hear something," Daphne said, "and it's not a ghost baby."

Sara heard the voices, talking low, and the scratching of a rat right by her foot.

"It's ghosts. I know it's ghosts. They're coming to get us because we're breaking the rules."

"I'm going back," Daphne said. "I'm not brave like you, Sara. I'm afraid."

"Come back with us, Sara," Jessica pleaded. "Come back with us."

But Sara didn't budge. She stood there and watched her friends run away. They were leaving her behind. She had to stay at Meyers Bickham but they were escaping.

And she didn't care about the ghosts. She didn't care if they carried her away. It would be better than staying here without her friends. Better than being so terribly lonely again.

But she was already alone. And the ghosts were coming. All in a line. Three of them carrying their laundry. She stood there in the shadows, watching, waiting for them to grab her and do whatever ghosts did to humans when they caught them in their world.

She couldn't see them clearly even though the one in front was carrying a lantern. They had coverings on their heads and were dressed all in black.

A horrid rat crawled onto her foot and she kicked it away. One of the ghosts turned and shined the beam of a flashlight straight into her face. They had seen her and they would take her away.

She ran, not stopping until she was up the stairs and back in her bed. But it was too late. The ghosts had seen her and one day they would come for her

*and carry her to the dark, musky basement to live
with them forever.*

That day was now.

"Help her out of there," Abigail ordered. "I have
better things than the remains of that disgusting basement in store for her."

One of the brutes half walked, half slid into the
basement with Sara, grabbed her arm and dragged
her back to where Abigail was waiting.

"It was you," Sara said, pushing closer to the doctor. "You saw me watching that night and you convinced me it was all a nightmare."

"You should have left it a nightmare, Sara. All
you had to do was keep quiet."

"You won't get away with this. Nat Sanderson
will know it's you. He'll make you pay. He will."

"That's the beauty of this, Sara. It won't matter
what he knows. He's going to die, too. Troy Wesley
will take care of that."

Sara tripped over a loose brick and fell to her
knees. Abigail stood over her, a silver pistol in her
hand. Behind her the cop and nurse imposters also
held guns. Pistols in their right hands, flashlights in
their left.

She expected them to shoot her and leave her for
the rats, but they were leaving the area now, walking
up the hill behind the orphanage. The would-be cop
walked beside her, his pistol pressed into the back of
her skull. They were going to kill her unless she
found some way to escape. Three against one. And
they were armed. The odds were not in her favor.

The beam of someone's flashlight slid across the
old storm cellar. A hole in the ground. Oh, no. She'd
peeked in there once. It was pitch-dark and smelled

of decaying earth. If they locked her in there, she might live for days. No food. No water. Just...

Big gray rats.

They'd crawl over her. They'd eat the flesh from her bones. And she'd be alive the whole time. Crying... Crying....

Sara spun around as the truth hit home. "It wasn't a ghost baby that cried in those walls, was it, Abigail? You buried a baby *alive*."

And now she was going to bury Sara the same way. Sara would never see Kendra again. Never see Nat again. Never tell him that she loved him.

"Open the door," Abigail ordered.

One of the doctor's trained goons did her bidding, swung out the door to the storm cellar while the other shoved Sara toward it. He shined his light into the hole. The rats scampered away, but they couldn't disappear. They just ran in circles as if they were frantically searching for escape or for food.

No doubt Abigail had them put there, her punishment to Sara for having seen too much. And Nat had been right all along. This was about more than unmarked graves of unidentified infants.

"You didn't just bury those babies, Abigail. You murdered them. What kind of sick, sadistic monster are you?"

"I didn't kill them. I just let them die. It was best for them."

"How can you say that? You're a doctor."

"You of all people should understand, Sara. They were flawed. No one would adopt them. No one wanted them. No one was ever going to want them."

"No one wanted me, Abigail, but I wanted to live."

"No one wanted either of us, but we weren't flawed. We didn't have handicaps. We didn't have to live our whole lives knowing no one would ever want us. Can't you see that would be worse than death?"

Sara shuddered. Abigail was beautiful, seemed to be sweet and caring, but beneath the facade she was evil. Evil, depraved and demented.

"Walk down the steps, Sara. Your grave is waiting. Or would you rather my friend here pushed you down?"

"My Kendra's not flawed, Abigail. She's perfect and she doesn't know anything that could hurt you. So don't hurt her. Please don't hurt Kendra."

"Down the steps."

But she didn't get time to take a step before she was pushed from the back and went tumbling into the black hole. She crawled up the steps, but the rats were already jumping at her feet. They would be all over her soon, nibbling at her neck, tangling in her hair.

She felt the claw of one through her pant leg. She screamed. So loud that she barely heard the door when it slammed shut and left her in pitch-darkness with the rodents.

Nat would find her. She knew he would. Troy Wesley would never outsmart Nat. He'd find her—but it would be too late.

Chapter Sixteen

Nat had been driving like crazy, heading north, finally reaching the county in the northwest section of Georgia where Troy Wesley was sheriff. He didn't know why he was here. The state police had been combing this area for the past three hours and were convinced the sheriff was nowhere around.

. Nat pulled over at a service station for a pit stop and a fill up. He took care of business and was about to rev up the bike when the cell phone rang.

"Hello."

"She's at Meyers Bickham."

"Wesley?"

"Yeah. Best if you sneak in. I doubt you'll come out alive, but that's your call."

"Who took them?"

But the connection was broken. Meyers Bickham. It was probably some kind of sick game. But he had no choice. And he was close. Real close. Almost as if fate had led him this way.

Only, the state police had been in the Meyers Bickham area half an hour ago. They should have seen something if Sara and Kendra or Wesley had been there.

Still, Nat called Bob Eggars to tell him where he was going. Bob promised to send someone out to meet him. Then Nat revved the engine and took off, flying down the highway, hating each second for ticking away before he reached the site of the old orphanage.

Nat did as Wesley suggested, sure he was heading into a trap, but not caring if it meant saving Sara and Kendra.

He killed his lights and engine and slunk through the trees on foot, knowing he was on the grounds of what had been Meyers Bickham but not sure exactly where the building had stood. He peered through the trees and saw the moonlight glint off the hood of a light-colored Jaguar. A black van was parked next to it. The vehicles were a good forty yards away.

He picked up his pace, running in that direction, hating that the limp slowed him down. And then he heard the scream. A piercing cry that tore through him like a hundred jagged-edged knives.

The scream didn't come from the direction of the vehicles, but from the opposite way. Nat saw a flash of light no more than thirty yards away. He cursed his leg, moving as fast as it would let him but staying in the trees until he was close enough to see two men standing on a hillside, both holding flashlights and pistols.

He stepped out of the shadows just before they reached him. "Put your hands up and drop those guns, unless one of you is eager to be a dead man."

One of them apparently was. Nat shot the pistol from his hand before the guy had the chance to aim it. He howled and started dancing around, holding his bloody hand and screaming obscenities.

The other guy threw his pistol to the ground and kicked it toward Nat.

"A smart move. Now you have two seconds to tell me where Sara is before I pull this trigger, and as you just saw, I won't miss."

"She's in the storm cellar," one of the men muttered. "Up the hill."

Nat picked up the two guns and took off toward the cellar as a second scream pierced the night and his soul. He grabbed the metal pull and yanked on the cellar door before he saw the lock. The men who had the key were probably nearly to their vehicles by now.

Nat wasn't waiting for another scream. He shot off the lock at an angle so that the bullet wouldn't penetrate the door. He got it open, knocked a huge rat from Sara's shoulder and pulled her up into his arms.

She held on for only a second before she tugged him away from the cellar. "I haven't seen Kendra since I was abducted from the hospital. We have to find her, Nat. We have to find her *now!*"

"Do you have any idea where she is?"

"No."

"Then let's get out of here."

"I don't think so."

Nat spun around and looked into the barrel of a silver pistol.

"Nice of you to join the party, Mr. Sanderson."

"Dr. Abigail Harrington," Sara said, "in case you're wondering who's holding the gun."

"Too bad you didn't notice me when you drove up," Abigail said. "I was using the outdoor facilities. Good timing on the part of my bladder, don't you think?"

"Great timing. Now why don't you put that gun away since your two heavyweights ran off and left you."

"I'm afraid that wouldn't be in my best interest. And it seems you've ruined the lock on the cellar door, Mr. Sanderson. Now I have no choice but to shoot you. I think you should go first, Sara. That way your crippled boyfriend can watch you die."

Now or never. There was no way Nat was going to just stand there and let her kill them. He watched her eyes, knew she wanted to kill them, but he also saw hesitancy. He'd have to get her talking again, then shove Sara to the ground and go for his own gun in one sweeping movement.

"Why did you kill Judge Arnold?"

"Because he's a sniveling coward who'd never keep his mouth shut."

Nat caught the movement of a big gray rat from the corner of his eye. It scuttled from the cellar and moved to Sara's foot.

"Any move will be her last."

Sara shook her head as the rat crawled onto her foot. "I don't think so, Abigail. I just don't think so."

Sara kicked and the huge gray rodent went flying through the air to hit Abigail's face. Nat threw himself in front of Sara as Abigail fired the pistol. But she was also clawing at the frightened rat with her long red fingernails, trying to get it to let go of her nose. The bullet missed them and ricocheted off the open cellar door.

Abigail's gun fell to the ground and Sara dived for it, then jumped up and pressed the weapon to the base of Abigail's skull as the rat finally let loose and scampered away.

"That's my woman," Nat said, smiling.

"I'm not a killer," Sara said, "but if I have to spend any more time around people like you I may learn to like it. Now if you don't want me to pull this trigger, you better talk fast. Where's my daughter?"

"There's a little redheaded girl who looks a lot like you asleep in a Jag back there." They all jumped at the sound of a male voice.

"About time you got here, Bob."

"You saw Kendra? She's okay?"

Sara handed the gun to Nat and went running toward the car.

"Let her go," Bob said, when Nat started to follow. "I checked the kid's pulse. She's fine, just sleeping. And a couple of state troopers should be pulling up just about now."

Nat saw the flashing lights through the trees.

"You look as if you've been busy here," Bob said, pulling a pair of handcuffs from the clamp at his waist.

"Just having a little trouble with rats. This two-legged one here's guilty of attempted murder and probably the murder of several unidentified infants and a judge. I'm not sure what else she's done, but I'm sure you'll find plenty to keep her in jail for the rest of her life."

"Her friend the sheriff will probably be doing a little time with her."

"If you find him."

"He called just after you did. Turned himself in

and promised to spill all the beans in exchange for a lighter sentence.''

''Are you bargaining with him?''

''That's yet to be decided. And here comes Bilks, so why don't you get out of here and let us take over,'' Bob said, closing the clamp on the handcuffs he'd already wrapped around Abigail's wrists.

Abigail muttered a string of curses and told Bob what he could do with his handcuffs.

''She's all yours,'' Nat said. ''But I have one little problem. I can't very well carry Sara and Kendra back with me on that stolen motorbike.''

''Stolen, huh? You *have* had a busy night. Take my car. I'll take the bike.''

''Thanks.''

''My pleasure. And take care of Sara. I've got a feeling she'd be real good to keep around for a long, long, time.''

''I've got a feeling you're right.''

IT WAS HOURS later when they finally got back to Nat's. They'd stopped at the emergency room on the way. The doctor on duty had checked the rat scratches on Sara's arms and legs, washed and treated them and given her a heavy duty antibiotic to ward off infection. He'd also assured them that rodents did not contract or transmit rabies.

Fortunately, even the scratches were minimal. The trousers had helped and the fact that Sara had stayed at the top of the narrow steps and kicked most of the frantic rodents away. But she wouldn't have fared nearly as well if Nat hadn't found her when he did.

The doctors checked out Kendra as well. She had been given a sedative when she'd been lured from the room and abducted. A small amount was still in her bloodstream but she'd woken while they were in the emergency room, perfectly happy and side-effect free without a clue as to the dangerous adventure she'd lived through.

She was asleep again now. Nat carried her into the house, waited while Sara turned down her covers. They both kissed her good-night and tiptoed from the room.

Nat pulled Sara into his arms in the hallway outside Kendra's room. It was already the wee hours of the morning, and he knew she was tired. Still, there were some things he needed to say. Some things she needed to hear.

"You were a real trooper today, Sara. You have been through all of this."

"I didn't want to be. I just wanted it all to go away."

"But you did what you had to do. You not only faced your past but stood up to everything they threw your way. I'm just sorry you had to go through so much. I promised to protect you, but I let you down."

"You couldn't have stopped it. I think it's been coming at me ever since that night when I heard the baby cry. And it wasn't going to stop until I collided full-force with the truth."

"But being locked in that storm cellar had to be terrifying."

"No more terrifying than the nightmares I've lived with for twenty years. And the scratches the rats left will heal completely."

"Hopefully you can put the nightmares behind you now."

"I think I can. And more. I think that finally the cries of the baby in the wall will grow silent." She pulled away and looked him in the eye. "What about you, Nat? Can you put your past behind you and go on with your life?"

He exhaled slowly, knowing that this was the moment of truth and wanting to be fully honest. "I'll never totally forgive myself for letting Maria's daughter get killed. It's not the sort of thing I can forget. But the recluse life is over. I'm ready to move on."

Nat pushed the hair back from her face and ran his fingers through it. "Did I ever tell you how beautiful you are, Sara?"

"That's going a little too far, Nat."

"No. I know you think you're plain, but I've never seen you that way. And the best part is you're not just beautiful on the outside, but deep inside, where it really counts. You're like the first apples in the fall, deliciously tempting, sweet and tart at the same time, a burst of flavor that just won't quit."

A FEW MINUTES AGO Sara had been so tired she'd had difficulty putting one foot in front of the other. She didn't feel that way now. She wasn't sure what was happening between her and Nat, but she knew that she loved him and felt that this was a moment she'd been moving toward all her life.

She rose to her tiptoes and kissed him, then pulled away and looked into his deep, dark eyes. Even with just the hall light dimly illuminating the living room, she could see something different in them. Less sadness. But they were as compelling as always, touching someplace deep inside where she'd never let anyone go before.

"I know you're tired, Sara."

"Not so much. But let's go to bed, Nat. I need a night in your arms. A night to do nothing but feel you next to me and not think of Meyers Bickham or ghosts or danger."

"Make that a couple of million nights, give or take ten, and you've got yourself a deal."

Sara trembled. "Do you know what you're asking, Nat?"

"Yeah. I know exactly what I'm asking and what I want. I want you and Kendra."

"We'll complicate your life."

"I hope so. I want it all. Complications. Responsibility. And love."

"Oh, you're going to get that, Apple Man. You are going to get that big time."

Sara melted against Nat's muscled chest as he lifted her in his arms and carried her to bed for the first of their few million nights. And when he kissed her, she knew that the curse of Meyers Bickham was finally over and a lifetime of true love was about to begin.

Epilogue

Four months later

The weather was perfect for the first ever Sanderson Orchards Apple Harvest Day. Mounds of whipped cream clouds floated in a sky of blue. The temperature hovered at sixty-five, and the wind that had swirled falling leaves into a frenzy yesterday had diminished to a titillating breeze.

Best of all, the grounds surrounding the rambling farmhouse teemed with people. Dorinda was manning the apple-bobbing, doing a great job with entertaining the clusters of laughing youngsters waiting their turn. The tables for the apple cider-tasting were crowded, too, keeping a fully recovered Raye Ann and Chatty Mattie—as Nat had teasingly dubbed her—very busy. And Henry and Blake were selling baskets of crisp red apples and jugs of Nat's home-made cider.

Nat was everywhere, answering questions about organic apple-growing. And Kendra and Mackie, the unofficial greeters, were here, there and all over the place, but mostly near the apple bobbers.

"Nat's good at this," Bob Eggars said, walking over to stand by Sara.

"I know. My husband is a constant surprise."

"Do you think he'll miss it?"

"A little, but not the way he's missed working with you guys. And we're not selling the orchard, just turning the operation of it over to Henry and Blake. We'll still be back here for vacations and to help with harvests when Nat's work permits."

"How do you feel about Nat's coming back to the Bureau?"

"Mixed emotions. I don't like the fact that he'll be dealing with dangerous psychos like Abigail Hoyt Harrington, but I know how important it is for him to do what he loves."

"And he'll be able to tackle it with no restraints now that his leg is only months away from a full recovery. Thanks to you."

"Nat was the one willing to undergo the surgery, painful recovery and the rehabilitation," Sara reminded him. "Even though there was only a fifty percent chance it would give him full use of the leg that had never healed right after he'd been shot."

"Yes, but you were with him every step of the way. No wonder he thinks you're the greatest thing since DNA testing."

"Since DNA testing? Ugh. That is soooo FBI. But I haven't given up my career, just postponed it. I'll go back one day, if and when I ever get tired of being a full-time wife and mother. But, for the record, I encouraged Nat to have the surgery—I didn't insist. There's no ordering Nat Sanderson around."

"Don't I know it. I always figured that was why he left the Bureau in the first place. There were just too many rules for him. But he's matured a lot since then. The Bureau's lucky to get him back.''

''And speaking of the Bureau, what's the latest on the case against Abigail?''

''Airtight. Not that juries haven't been known to throw out all relevant evidence and go for a pretty face and winning smile, but I can't see that happening with a pediatrician who murdered babies.''

''And buried at least one of them alive.''

''That one act pretty much seals her fate, though even Wesley says that was an accident. The infant was seizuring almost constantly, and when she went into a coma after a particularly severe one, the caretakers thought she was dead. When they called Abigail, she told them to go ahead and bury her.''

Sara shook her head. ''Irresponsibility on every level. That was Meyers Bickham, right down to a security guard who used a pick ax to dig graves in the basement wall.''

''And you and your friends happened to be in the basement on what was hopefully the only night a baby had been buried alive. If you hadn't heard its cries, we might never have known how those bodies got there.''

''Nat says Abigail was actually the instigator of the scheme to falsify adoption records as well.''

''But Cary Arnold went along with it, and so did the late Senator Marcus Hayden and his wife Sheila who were working there at the time,'' Bob said. ''Apparently they made quite a team. A total absence of conscience amongst all of them.''

''And they ended up as a senator, a prestigious and socially prominent doctor and a federal judge,'' Sara said.

Nat walked up and put his arms around Sara, stroking the barely imperceptible swell of her tummy with the palms of his hands. "You two look awfully glum," Nat said. "Hope you're not filling my wife's head with FBI horror tales."

"Me?" Bob managed a shocked expression. "I was just asking for her apple pie recipe."

"Sure you were."

"Actually we were discussing how society rewards moral depravity," Sara said, "as evidenced by the success of Marcus Hayden, Abigail Harrington and Cary Arnold."

"All depends on how you measure success," Nat said. "I have serious doubts any of them were ever as happy as I am right now. A beautiful wife, an adorable stepdaughter and a bun in the oven, as Henry puts it. Plus we can sleep at night knowing we didn't sell our souls to the devil in exchange for a few dollars."

"When you look at it that way, success at any price just may be the ultimate failure," Sara said.

"And while we're on the disgusting subject of MB, what is the current score?"

"Definitely need a scorecard to follow this one, but Abigail's still winning. She let the babies whose bodies were buried in the basement die by not giving appropriate medical care and letting them be buried without an autopsy. And she had her bought and paid for goons kill Judge Arnold."

"But Nat said it was Judge Arnold who attacked Raye Ann," Sara said.

"Yeah. The guy didn't do his homework the way Abigail did. He thought you were still living in the apartment and meant to frighten you into keeping quiet, the same way he did in the ladies' room in Dahlonega when he followed you and Nat. The guy was apparently running so scared he lost all perspective. Which is no doubt why Abigail had him killed. She thought he might get out of hand.''

"As if she wasn't," Nat added, "with her threats and house-burning antics.''

"And now we're looking into the possibility that she may have murdered one of the former MB caretakers, who died in a suspicious house fire a few years back.''

"Was Troy Wesley in on all of that with her?" Sara asked.

"He definitely knew about the babies. Abigail and Cary bought his silence by helping him get elected. He was going to cover up the findings in the investigation until the FBI got invited to the dance. I think he was still prepared to do all he could to cover it up when Abigail ordered him to kill Nat. He balked at that point and called Nat instead. Then he turned himself in.''

"A strange group of bedfellows," Nat said. "All tangled in the same filthy sheets.''

"You're right," Sara agreed. "What a web they spun. No wonder they all got caught in it.''

"And that's enough shop talk," Nat said, kissing her on the back of her neck.

"I never got the apple pie recipe," Bob said. They all laughed.

Nat kept his arms around Sara as Bob headed back to the cider-tasting table. "You're not still nervous are you?"

"A little," she admitted. "I haven't seen Jessica or Daphne—who's now called Caroline—in twenty years. What if we've all changed so much that we just stand around staring at each other, trying to imagine why we were ever friends?''

"You, Sara Murdoch Sanderson, at a loss for words! That will be the day.''

"All the same, having them come here today could be a disaster.''

"Can't be a total disaster. We'll make them buy apples.''

"You!'' She turned to give him a playful punch, but he caught her in his arms and kissed her. She was still reeling from the effects when he put his mouth to her ear. "Don't look now,'' he whispered, "but I think your friends have just arrived.''

Sara spun and stared at the two couples walking toward them. Jessica and Caroline with men who must be their husbands, Conner and Sam. Even without the photos they'd exchanged via e-mail, Sara was certain she would have recognized the two women.

Her doubts were forgotten as she rushed toward them. They fell into each other's arms, laughing and squealing and hugging as if they were ten again. Holding on to each other the way they had that night in the dark basement, but this time without the fear.

Three friends from Meyers Bickham. Reunited in a world that was beautiful and overflowing with love. And Sara had the crazy feeling that somewhere above them an angel baby who'd once cried in a dark, cold basement wall was looking down on them and smiling.

The cries had finally been silenced by justice, friendship and the miracle of love.

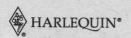
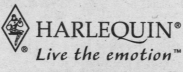

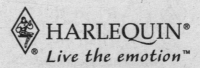

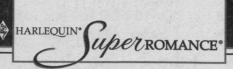

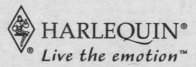

Harlequin Romance®

THE WEDDING PLANNERS

Where weddings are all in a day's work!

Have you ever wondered about the women behind the
scenes, the ones who make those special days happen, the
ones who help to create a memory built on love that lasts
forever—who, no matter how expert they are at helping
others, can't quite sort out their love lives for themselves?

Meet Tara, Skye and Riana—three sisters whose jobs consist
of arranging the most perfect and romantic weddings
imaginable—and read how they find themselves walking
down the aisle with their very own Mr. Right…!

**Don't miss the THE WEDDING PLANNERS trilogy
by Australian author Darcy Maguire:**

A Professional Engagement HR#3801
On sale June 2004 in Harlequin Romance®!

Plus:

The Best Man's Baby, HR#3805, on sale July 2004
A Convenient Groom, HR#3809, on sale August 2004

Available at your favorite retail outlet.

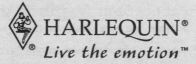

HARLEQUIN®
Live the emotion™

Visit us at www.eHarlequin.com

HRTWP

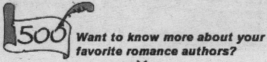

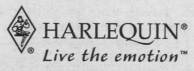